
★ ---

A TALENT FOR MURDER

He lay on his stomach, bluejeaned legs splayed, yellow sweater with more crusty brown...

Adam pushed past Joanna. She backed up against the wall. He knelt, blocking her view of the man on the floor, grabbing his wrist.

Joanna sucked in her breath, closed her eyes, fought for equilibrium. Opened them again and focused on the sofa bed. Light blue jacket... down jacket...light blue down jacket with a rip in the pocket that he should have mended but he didn't and I only gave it to him last Christmas and now he's...

"E.J.!"

Adam pivoted, face shocked and drained. He reached for her, but she pushed him aside. Stared down into the face of the dead man.

Not E.J.

Antony Parducci.

--- ★ ---

"A suspenseful Joanna Stark mystery."
—*San Francisco Examiner-Chronicle*

"Muller ties all the loose ends neatly together." —*Publishers Weekly*

DARK STAR

MARCIA MULLER

WORLDWIDE®

TORONTO • NEW YORK • LONDON • PARIS
AMSTERDAM • STOCKHOLM • HAMBURG
ATHENS • MILAN • TOKYO • SYDNEY

DARK STAR

A Worldwide Mystery/October 1990

First published by St. Martin's Press Incorporated.

ISBN 0-373-26058-X

Printed in U.S.A.

For Mary McCarthy Fredrick

ONE

THE WINERY LOOKED like an ancient monastery—after the Huns had sacked it.

Joanna Stark brought her car to a stop and stared in dismay at the dark stone building. Its massive wooden doors leaned open at peculiar angles, their hinges broken. The roofline sagged. Ivy crawled up the walls, blocking the windows and seizing the rusted flagpole that jutted out over the entry in a stranglehold. She'd had to maneuver her Fiat around rocks and potholes all the way from the main highway; the retaining wall on either side of the access road was crumbling. The only positive signs were the grapevines that covered the surrounding hillsides. The only signs of human habitation were the motorcycle and two pickups in the parking area. Those, and the cheerful whistling that came from inside the building.

Good God, she thought, what have I sunk my money into?

The lilting tune went on, her whistling son happily oblivious to his major investor's horror.

It wasn't as if Joanna hadn't seen the place before, but that had been the previous summer, with E.J. and the real estate broker. In the ten months since then she'd steered clear of the complicated purchase negotiations, on the theory that if you are lending your child a goodly sum of money in the hope that it will help him to become a grownup, you'd damned well better treat him like one. Besides, during the initial showing of the property E.J. had been high on the prospect of buying his own winery, and the broker—sly, dissembling creature that she was—had waxed enthusiastic. Joanna had been caught up in their mood, buoyed along by relief that her peripatetic son might finally be settling down to his life's work. But now...

"He'll need *nine* lives to accomplish what needs to be done here," she muttered grimly.

After a moment she got out of the car and removed from the trunk the picnic basket containing a special lunch assembled to celebrate E.J.'s first day in possession of the winery. She carried it to a broken-down table under an oak tree at the corner of the building, left it there, and went toward the double doors, calling out. E.J.'s voice replied, somewhat muffled.

The building was dark and cold inside—a decided contrast to the fine April day. Its thick walls trapped musty air characteristic of wineries the world over: redolent of oak barrels and fermented grapes, sweet-sour and not at all unpleasant, telling of a long line of vintages tended by generations of loving hands. Joanna breathed in deeply.

The large, high-ceilinged room, which eventually would be the tasting area, was crowded with packing cases. Straight ahead was another massive wooden door that led into the actual workaday winery. To the left was an ornately carved L-shaped bar, also piled with cartons. E.J.'s elfin bearded face looked out from between two of the piles, and then he came around the bar, a broom in one hand. He wore his oldest jeans and a workshirt with a tattered tail, and his blond curls were held back by a red sweatband.

"It must be lunchtime," he said.

"Yes, I've brought your inaugural picnic." She looked around, noting that the previous owners had left behind the sepia-toned old-time photographs of the town of Sonoma and the Valley of the Moon. And also noting the mud-caked floor, water-stained walls, and moldy wine casks. "Uh, how's it going?" she asked.

E.J. smiled and leaned the broom against the bar. "Not too bad, but I think I need a mop. I'm going to run into town later for cleaning supplies."

At least he hadn't asked to borrow her mop, Joanna thought. Becoming a man of property was already having a positive effect on him. She took a final look around and said, "I think a fire hose would be more in order."

He grinned more widely and ruffled her curls—as dark as his were light. "Oh, come on, Jo. It's not that bad."

And maybe it wasn't, she thought. E.J. certainly didn't seem worried. Maybe to one with the boundless energy of twenty-three the cleanup job was a piece of cake. But what about the myriad other improvements that must be made before he could actually embark on the winemaking process...?

E.J. proudly handed her her set of keys to the winery— major investor's privilege—and propelled her out to the picnic table, where he pawed through the basket, exclaiming because she'd brought all his favorites: sourdough still warm from the Sonoma French Bakery; garlic jack and Brie from the Cheese Factory; salami and pepperoni from the Sausage Company; a good Buena Vista zinfandel. Joanna liked to cook, but not for picnics; for those she preferred to make a quick shopping blitz around the town plaza. Sonoma—a small old town nestled in one of California's prime grape-growing valleys some forty miles north of San Francisco—attracted tourists from all over the world for good reason; its shops were numerous and varied, many of them chock-full of wonderful things to eat and drink.

While she opened the wine, E.J. unpacked the food and set out three paper plates and napkins. "Joe'll be joining us in a few minutes," he said.

Joe Donatello was the youngest in a long line of valley vintners, a man of twenty-five who had already achieved a certain reputation in the wine industry. He and E.J. had been friends for over a year and, Joanna suspected, it was

Joe who had first encouraged her son to try his hand at the business. In spite of that, she'd been surprised when E.J. had announced that Joe was joining the fledgling Elliot J. Stark Vineyards as winemaker. The valley vintners guarded talent as jealously as they did turf; the fact that Joe had turned his back on the Donatello family business hinted at a schism as serious as those that had previously split such well-known clans as the Sebastianis and the Napa Valley's Mondavis.

She was about to ask E.J. what he knew of Joe's personal situation when she heard footsteps approaching on the path that led around the winery. The winemaker—barefoot and wearing only grubby cutoffs—emerged from the tangled underbrush. He was black haired and compactly built; his tanned musculature reminded Joanna of bronzes created by the fifteenth-century sculptor of the same last name. And, she thought, Joe was just as much of an artist, creating masterpieces to delight the palate rather than the eye.

He waved and went to his pickup, which was parked behind the winery's rattletrap white truck, then ambled toward them, pulling on a shirt. "Christ, it's filthy back there," he said. "We're going to have to put in that shower right away, or we'll be running back to our former homes twice a day to get cleaned up."

"You're moving in here with E.J., then?"

"Yeah." Joe sat down and reached for a piece of sourdough.

When Joanna looked at E.J., his eyes were focused determinedly on the sandwich he was constructing. He knew she felt torn about his moving out of the farmhouse they shared in Sonoma, some ten miles down the valley. It wasn't that she resented his independence—he'd always exercised plenty of that—but just a year ago she'd been involved in some very bad things that had left her unsure of herself and fearful. She realized that was the reason E.J. was moving to the winery: He considered it time she exorcised her fear, and knew the only way she could do so was as she always had—alone. But the realization didn't make his going any easier.

It was odd, she reflected now, when the child revealed himself as more wise than the parent, started to look out for the one who had always looked out for him. And it was especially odd when the parent was only forty-three.

Now E.J. glanced nervously at her. She knew that look: He was afraid she was brooding. Since she didn't want to spoil this celebratory picnic, she shoved these thoughts to the back of her mind and said to Joe, "So how are things in your bailiwick?"

"Like I said, it's filthy." He motioned at the L-shaped wing projecting from the rear of the winery, where the winemaker's laboratory was. "The equipment's arrived, thanks to your generous check, but I don't dare unpack it until I get the mess cleaned up." To E.J. he added, "I think we could use a mop."

"I was thinking along those lines myself. I'm going to town later for cleaning stuff."

"Why not let me pick it up?" Joe looked at his watch. "I'm meeting Karla Perelli at two."

"The wine broker?" Joanna asked. Karla Perelli served as a marketing agent for small wineries—those with annual sales of less than 100,000 cases—that did not maintain their own sales force.

"Yeah. She's a friend. I want to talk to her about our plans. She doesn't usually take on an account this early in the game, but for us I think she'll make an exception."

Joe's easy, confident smile left Joanna with no doubt that he would succeed in securing the pretty young broker's representation; Karla was said to have a fondness for the occasional oddball account—and for handsome men. "How does it work?" she asked. "She buys the wine outright from you?"

"Right. Then she markets it at her own price, providing all the advertising and promotion. What interests me most

is her ability to build a winery's image. E.J. and I agree we
have to get rolling on that early, to overcome Sonoma's ob-
scurity factor.''

Joanna understood exactly what he meant. While the
state of California encompasses a number of prime winemaking areas, those who are unfamiliar with the industry
tend to think of it only in terms of the Napa Valley. Small
vintners in less well known locales suffer by comparison,
and in Sonoma County the problem is further complicated
by the existence—in the French manner—of a number of
smaller grape-growing districts, such as Chalk Hill, Alexander Valley, Russian River, Sonoma Mountain. In recent
years Joanna had noticed an increase in local resentment
toward the Napa Valley's dominance; many Sonomans
charged the Napa vintners with snobbery and living off
largely unfounded reputations. Napans, on the other hand,
criticized Sonomans for having chips on their shoulders or—
worst of all—sour grapes. Joanna was glad to see E.J. and
Joe doing something about the problem, rather than simply complaining.

Joe seemed to interpret her silence as skepticism about
their immediate need for a wine broker. He said, "Really,
this place isn't in as bad a shape as it looks. The new tanks
and presses are being delivered this afternoon. We've got
some of the best planted acreage around. Those vines are
well established, and what we can't grow I've already con-
tracted to buy. By this time next year, people'll be talking
about Stark Vineyards. In a few years we'll be a force to be
reckoned with.'' He paused, pepperoni-laden bread raised
triumphantly. His eyes moved from Joanna's face to E.J.'s,
and he grinned sheepishly. "Well, we will if I remember to
buy the mop."

"*Two* mops," E.J. said.

"And buckets," Joanna added.

"...Right. What's good for real dirty floors?"

"Try Spic and Span."

Joe nodded.

Joanna poured herself some more wine. The alcohol had unleashed her natural nosiness, and she decided to pry a little. "I guess your grandfather's going to be lonely, with you leaving both the house and winery, and Veronica going off to Washington."

Joe scowled. "She's not a congresswoman yet; the election's not until next Tuesday."

"The last poll I saw said she has the edge."

"Polls have been known to be wrong."

"You don't want your sister elected?"

Joe shrugged irritably and bit into his sandwich.

The Donatellos, while maintaining a lower profile than many of their vintner neighbors, had always been politically powerful. For fifteen years Joe's older sister Veronica had championed the causes of the growers—first on the county board of supervisors and lately in the state senate. Now a seat in the U.S. House of Representatives had been vacated by the death of the incumbent, and Veronica was a major contender for it. The campaign for the upcoming special election had been brief, spirited, and—in accordance with Veronica's usual tactics—fairly dirty.

Joanna could understand Joe—who, from her previous observations, seemed unusually idealistic, even naive—taking exception to his sister's methods. And in view of his break with the family, it didn't strike her as odd that he wasn't standing on a street corner passing out campaign literature. But the degree of bitterness in his voice took her aback.

Joe seemed to sense her reaction. He said more gently, "Look, Ronnie and I don't see eye to eye politically. Actually, politics do nothing for me. I'm like E.J.—just want to make some wine, smoke some dope, chase some women, and have the politicians leave me the hell alone."

Joanna sighed. She herself was reasonably apolitical, but she'd hoped for more from her son's generation.

Joe wolfed the rest of his sandwich, drank off his wine, and stood. "I might as well pick up the cleaning stuff before I go see Karla." To Joanna he added, "Are you going to be around for a while?"

"For an hour or so. I want to get home by two-thirty. My business partner's coming at three."

"Too bad—I was going to offer to show you some of the equipment you paid for when I get back."

"Save it for my next visit. It'll be safe to unpack it then."

Joe nodded and was about to speak when there was the sound of a car on the access road. A tan Jaguar sedan pulled into the parking area and stopped behind the pickups.

The winemaker said softly, "Oh shit."

The white-haired man who got out of the car had the same compact build and strong Italian features as Joe. Although he looked to be in his seventies, he moved with brisk agility. His sports clothes spoke both of money and a concern with his appearance. This, Joanna thought, must be Robert Donatello, family patriarch and the grandfather who had raised Joe and Veronica.

The winemaker's introduction proved her guess to be correct. Donatello greeted her cordially, then nodded at E.J. and congratulated him on his purchase of the winery. If the old man bore a grudge against him for luring his grandson away from the family enterprise, he was masking it well. The pleasantries over, he said, "Joey, I've got to talk to you."

"All right." Joe waited, arms folded across his chest.

"Could we go inside?" Donatello motioned at the double doors of the winery.

Joe hesitated, then shrugged and led his grandfather away.

When they were out of earshot, Joanna said, "What do you suppose he wants?"

"He's probably going to try to talk Joe into coming back into the fold." E.J. spoke offhandedly, but his eyes were clouded with worry.

"He wouldn't let you down now."

"No. Joe's dependable—plus we've signed a two-year contract." E.J. divided the remainder of the wine between them. For a few minutes they ate in silence. Then he said, "Nick's coming up today?"

"Yes. We need to go over the books, and then he'll stay to dinner."

Nick Alexander was her partner in Security Systems International, a San Francisco firm that provided security services to museums and art galleries. Joanna's participation in the business ranged from vigorous to practically nonexistent, depending on her mood and personal circumstances. During the past year she'd pretty much stayed away from their Market Street offices, but since she still held a considerable financial stake in the company and Nick was a poor-to-awful manager, she'd recently decided she'd better look into how things were going.

E.J. nodded approvingly. "Be sure to cook enough for three." He liked Nick. And, she suspected, he liked the idea of her becoming involved in the business again even better.

Irritation flickered within her, not at the thought of fixing dinner for three—she'd planned on that—but at her son's approbation. It struck her as faintly condescending; she half expected him to pat her on the head and call her a good girl. Sullenly she said, "I'm only going over the books with him. It doesn't mean I plan to go back to work."

E.J. sipped wine, saying nothing.

"Why should I work, anyway? It isn't as if I need the money."

He shrugged.

"Well, it isn't. David left me altogether too well provided for—you know that. I might as well take the spring and summer off and enjoy myself. I put in that damned swimming pool last year and it's only been used for part of one season. Now that you're moving out I can barely justify the expense of the solar heating..." She let her words trail off, realizing how ridiculous it sounded to be carping about running the solar equipment when she'd just said she didn't need to work.

E.J. set his glass down and placed one hand over hers. "You've got to let go sometime," he said.

"What's that supposed to—" She paused as Robert Donatello came out of the winery, waved to them, and went to his Jaguar. Moments later Joe emerged and got into his red pickup. The two drove off in tandem, Joe calling out thanks for the lunch.

E.J. was looking worried again, but Joanna wasn't willing to let his earlier remark pass. "What do you mean, let go?" she asked. "I let you go at birth, when I handed you over to David and Eleanor for adoption. Even after I married him I didn't exactly clutch at you. It was *my* idea to let you go on thinking they were your natural parents. And since you've known the truth—"

"Jo, I'm not talking about letting go of me."

"What, then?"

"You've got to let go of the fear that my father is going to come back and harm us."

"I don't—"

"Yes, you do. You don't really believe Parducci died last year in Cornwall. But he *did*, Jo. Antony Parducci is dead."

They stared at one another—eyes steady, hands touching, at the same stalemate in the same argument they'd been having for the past eleven months.

E.J. was right, Joanna thought; she had to let go of the fear, because it was crippling her. But E.J. was also wrong: Antony Parducci had *not* died in the icy waters of the River Fal the previous May. Although she couldn't prove it, she was absolutely certain that the art thief, her former lover, was still alive.

TWO

JOANNA ARRIVED at the farmhouse on Old Winery Road at twenty to three, her white Fiat convertible laden with groceries. On the trip down the valley she'd mentally fussed over what to fix for dinner, and when she'd swung into Safeway's parking lot she still had no plan. It was in the liquor section that a display of Tsing Tao beer gave her inspiration: Chinese food. Nick loved Chinese; so did E.J. Joanna loved it, too, but seldom cooked it because of the cutting and dicing and chopping involved. But tonight, with two additional pairs of hands to help, a veritable feast would be theirs.

She loaded her cart with Tsing Tao, chicken, wonton wrappers, cilantro, shrimp, and all manner of exquisite mushrooms and roots and shoots. Then she threw in a cooked crab for good measure and drove home, humming happily.

The house was a Victorian: sparkling white with a wraparound porch and gingerbreading, set back from the road on a big double lot. The persimmon tree in front—which seemed to double in size every year—screened it from the prying eyes of tourists en route to the tasting room at Buena Vista Winery. Through a line of slender white birch saplings the aquamarine of the new swimming pool shimmered. Joanna slowed the car, feeling a flush of pride that had not diminished after four-plus years. She loved the house; it was the first nice thing of her own that she'd ever had.

The house had originally belonged to an uncle of David's; her husband had inherited it less than a year before his death from cancer. After David's funeral Joanna had fled San Francisco—his greedy, angry relatives and too many memories speeding her departure—with the idea of opening an art gallery in Sonoma. But in the end, instead of adding another shop to a tourist town amply supplied with them, she let the house become her labor of love, transforming it from an unsightly derelict to one of the grand old ladies of the valley. Her pride was fully justified: The work she'd done herself and her supervision of what her best friend called the "goon squads" had not been easy.

And by virtue of that, even though unearned wealth did not sit well on her puritanical shoulders, the house had become hers alone.

Because of the number of grocery bags, she drove around to the kitchen door rather than leaving the car in the circular drive and entering through the front. The air inside was hot and close; she set the first sack down and opened windows. Herman, the stray black cat she'd taken in the previous spring, looked lazily up at her from his favorite place on the counter next to the coffee maker. She scooped him up and dropped him on the floor with a thud—not an inconsiderable one, given his girth. Ermine, his white counterpart who had been adopted from a service called Pets' Lifeline to keep Herman company (and, she hoped, to teach him better manners), looked up from the cat basket in the corner and yawned. Joanna patted Herman, who sat lumpishly at her feet looking hurt. Then she felt guilty toward Ermine, and went to pat him, too. Somehow she'd never quite warmed up toward him; the goddamned cat was a sycophant.

Maybe, she thought as she fetched the other groceries, she could talk E.J. into taking the cats to live at the winery. But she wasn't sure she could stand to be parted from Herman, wicked ways and all, and Herman would pine away without Ermine...God, why did life have to be complicated even on the level of pets?

At any rate, she'd have to remember to put Herman out-doors before Nick arrived. The animal hated all men but E.J. His favorite ploy was to hide behind the furniture and wait until they passed, then rush out and bite them on the ankles.

The groceries stowed away, she glanced at the kitchen clock. Three-oh-five; Nick was late, which wasn't surprising. She sat down at the round table in the breakfast nook and pulled her favorite Chinese cookbook from the shelf under the window. After she'd familiarized herself with the recipes she—no, *they*—would follow, she got up and wandered through the dining room to the front parlor. She'd recently suffered a fit of rearranging, and she wasn't sure if she really liked the couch at a right angle to the fireplace...

She moved to the front window and peered out. No blue Mustang, no Nick. There was a redwood burl table beneath the window—a piece that David and his first wife Eleanor had acquired on vacation in Oregon. David—usually a man of fine taste—had loved the burl for some inexplicable reason, and that, coupled with Joanna's guilt toward Eleanor, had prevented her from getting rid of it. Instead she attempted to disguise it with leafy plants and a few choice knickknacks.

When she looked down she saw her fat pottery pony, a souvenir of her last abortive trip to England; it was lying on the hardwood floor, one leg broken off. Exclaiming in dismay, she stooped and picked it up, then whirled to look for Herman. When something got mysteriously broken, the cat was usually not far away.

No Herman. He'd probably heard her come in here and made himself scarce. She set the pony and its severed leg on the coffee table and went to the front hall where she kept an assortment of glues in the hall chair for Herman-perpetrated disasters.

But she paused with her hand on the chair's hinged seat, staring at the wall across from her. The hall was her private art gallery; her favorite and most valuable paintings hung there, protected from fading rays of sun and temperature extremes. Favorite and most valuable, with one exception.

And it was that one—*Stark's Dark Star*—that was missing.

Her breath caught and she straightened. Frantically she scanned the wall, thinking she must be mistaken.

No, there were an empty space and picture hook where *Dark Star* had hung.

Nothing else—the small Rodriguez, the Picasso drawing, the Hopper, the Matisse, or the Gorman—was missing.

Only the worthless painting was gone.

The worthless painting that symbolized her own foolhardiness—and whose creation had set in motion the events that had resulted in her present fear-crippled state.

The only person who could possibly have a reason for stealing *Dark Star* was Antony Parducci. And he would not have done so because he wanted the painting itself. His purpose would have been to give Joanna a sign that he was alive . . . perhaps even to challenge her.

Antony Parducci had been here in her own home, today!

Joanna's heart began to hammer as she stood, fists clenched, eyes on the empty picture hook. Then she turned and went back to the living room. It looked the same as it had minutes before, but now her sharpened senses detected something she hadn't noticed. An odor? No. An emotional aura, the sense of violation? Perhaps. But something more. What?

Her gaze moved to the broken-legged pony on the coffee table. Drifted to the redwood burl table where the pony customarily stood under the trailing fronds of a fern. Slowly she went over there, squatted down, and felt along the smoothly varnished surface.

Her fingers encountered a familiar cardboard shape. A matchbook. She never kept matchbooks there. She pulled it from under the fronds. Held it up and read the inscription.

The Greenbank Hotel, Falmouth, Cornwall.

Joanna rocked back on her heels, sat down hard on the floor. Her fingers curled around the matchbook as dark visions flooded her mind.

A towering bank of fog, hovering over the River Fal...black swiftly moving water, ripples gleaming in the light from a ship...Antony Parducci, his eyes coldly calculating...

She remembered sounds, too: a boat thumping against a barge...a throbbing engine...the splash of a body going over the side...

She uncurled her fingers and looked closely at the matchbook. The Greenbank Hotel was where she had been staying at the time of her last encounter with Parducci. She assumed he'd known she was there, might have stopped in to ask about her and pocketed these matches. The book was creased, nearly flattened; the tips of the matches themselves had crumbled away, the striking surface had peeled off. The printing was blurred by water stains.

A matchbook that had been left a long time in the pocket of a water-soaked garment would look like this.

A curious calm descended on Joanna. She'd known all along that something like this would eventually happen; the knowledge had prepared her to deal with the shock. The missing painting and the presence of this matchbook constituted a message from Parducci.

I'm alive and close by. Catch me if you can, before I catch you.

But this was no playful dare, no child's game of hide-and-seek. Parducci was attempting to lure her out so he could kill her. He'd tried it before.

The man was insane. He'd killed others and, having acquired a taste for it, was now bent on destroying the woman who had denied him access to his son and had almost put him behind bars. He would not do it immediately; if that were his plan he would have waited for her here in the house. Instead he would draw it out, until her nerve broke, until he had made her insane, too.

After a moment she got up and placed the matchbook next to the broken pony on the coffee table. Automatically she went through the house, checking the locks on the doors, the fastenings on the windows. She'd always been security-conscious—given her partnership in SSI and the value of her art collection—but life in Sonoma often tempted her to become lax. Now she went over the house thoroughly, but was unable to find how Parducci had gained entry.

She was descending from the second floor when she heard a car's engine out front. By the time she reached the door, Nick Alexander stood on the front porch.

Nick was tall and gaunt, with a lined, craggy face and thick gray black hair. Today he wore Banana Republic khakis and an Indian cotton shirt, with a snap-brim jungle hat that obviously came from the same outfitter. Normally Joanna would have been amused by his city-person's idea of what was suitable attire for visiting in Sonoma, but now she merely smiled absently at him and accepted the shopping bag he held out. It contained a great sheaf of computer printout and two bottles of wine.

Nick stepped into the hall and watched her double-lock the door. His bushy eyebrows pulled together as she secured the chain. When she still didn't speak he said, "How have you been lately, Nick? Oh, fine, thank you."

Now she frowned in return.

"Thank you for the wine, Nick," he went on. "Oh, you're welcome, Joanna. It's a nice little vintage that I picked up down the road—which is why I'm late."

"Oh God, I'm sorry!" she said. "Don't mind me—it's been a strange day."

She led him to the kitchen, asked what kind of wine he'd like, and went to work with the corkscrew. All the time she was trying to decide how much to reveal to him. Nothing, she concluded.

The habit of secrecy was so deeply ingrained in her that she had difficulty confiding in even those closest to her. And Nick, in spite of their long-standing partnership, was a friend whom she preferred to keep at an arm's length. He was unaware of her personal relationship with Antony Parducci, did not know that E.J. was the art thief's son. In fact, he considered her preoccupation with apprehending Parducci an aberration bordering on the deranged. Joanna did not want to hear one of his lectures to that effect—not now, not in her present emotional state.

"So what was so strange about today?" Nick asked.

"Oh...I guess it's just odd seeing E.J. as owner of a winery, and knowing he'll be moving out of the house. And the winery itself...you really ought to talk him into giving you a tour—after they've scraped the mud off the floors." She paused. "Look, Nick, would you mind very much if we just have a nice dinner tonight and skip going over the books? You can leave the printout with me and after I've gone over it, I'll drive down to the city—"

"I was hoping you'd see your way to coming in to the office soon. What's for dinner?"

"Chinese. We're fixing it—you, E.J., and me." She was about to hand him a cleaver and put him to work when the phone rang.

It was E.J., sounding harried. "Listen, what time is dinner?"

"Not for quite a while. You're helping fix it."

"Oh. Well, I'll be there as soon as I can. My keys are missing, so I can't start either the bike or the winery truck, and Joe's off at the building supply in Santa Rosa. I'll probably have to hitch home."

Joanna was silent, thinking of that key ring. Besides E.J.'s motorcycle keys, it contained a full set of house keys, both to this place and her apartment in the city.

"I'm sure they're around someplace," E.J. added. "We've been moving stuff ever since Joe got back from seeing Karla, and they probably got shoved behind some boxes."

Or, she thought, they had been taken and used to gain entry to her house. But that was ridiculous: Parducci couldn't have known about the winery, much less just walked in there and appropriated the keys. Unless he was keeping very close tabs on her and E.J. Unless he had totally altered his appearance....

"E.J.," she said, "has anyone been there today besides you and Joe and his grandfather?"

"Sure. Delivery people. Why?"

"Uh, no reason." Her protective instincts toward her son had always run high. There was no way she would confide her fears until she was certain they were grounded. "Look for the keys a while longer, and if you don't find them, Nick or I will come fetch you."

With typical independence, E.J. said, "No, I'll just hitch," and hung up.

Joanna put Nick to work cutting up the chicken while she fed vegetables to the Cuisinart. She kept up a steady stream of mundane chatter, trying to direct her thoughts away from Parducci. While his image remained close to the forefront of her consciousness, she found that in time she could relax—so much so that when Herman streaked out from behind the chopping block and planted a fang in Nick's ankle, she laughed uproariously, then had to act contrite and embarrassed while her partner hopped around on one foot and cursed the furry fiend. Further relief was provided by the sound of E.J.'s bike and his announcement that the keys had indeed been shoved behind a pile of packing cases. By the time Nick left at eleven, Joanna felt vaguely optimistic about getting a decent night's sleep.

Sleep was important: She needed to be fresh and alert in the morning when she began to tackle the problem of Antony Parducci's resurrection.

THREE

APRIL MORNINGS in the Sonoma Valley have the power to lure both the most dedicated workers and confirmed sluga-beds out of doors. While the day may dawn crisp, by the time the sun touches the tops of the gravevines an enticing warmth sets in. Protected from the wind-driven ocean fogs of the West Marin and Sonoma headlands, as well as the tule fogs that rise from the marshes along the Petaluma River, the valley would seem a perfect breeding ground for indolence. But its residents know that as noon approaches the sun's rays may cause discomfort, so most of them go about their business early, with vigor.

Not so with Joanna, however. She usually liked to drink coffee on her patio, where she could page idly through the San Francisco paper and enjoy the fragrance of whatever was in bloom out there—lately, the citrus trees. Eleven or twelve was time enough to make the half-mile trip into town (by car these days—she'd suffered enough bruises and wrenched knees to realize she'd never be an adequate bi-cyclist) to pick up her mail at the post office, run errands, chat with friends, and lunch at one of the cafés or restau-rants around the plaza. For close to a year hers had been an ordered yet essentially purposeless existence regulated by the rhythm of a routine that included gardening, swimming, reading, and simply basking in the sun. An existence pecu-liarly at odds with her internal state of perpetual unease.

But with the disappearance of *Dark Star*, the unease had been transformed into a steadily throbbing dread. Yester-day's lazy mornings were now unthinkable.

Nine o'clock on Thursday found her seated at a window table in her favorite coffeehouse, French roast to hand, waiting for Sally Jane Lane. Sally Jane was a reporter for the biweekly *Index-Tribune*, and, in spite of the girlish rhyming name, a tough journalist who covered everything from fiftieth wedding anniversary parties to massive drug busts with an exacting professionalism. The paper itself contained a curious melange of small-town news items (wedding notices, high school sports, social notes, club news) and stories on such major issues as controlled growth and industrialization, crime, and recently the special election campaigns for the vacated House seat.

Joanna had once bought the local paper mainly for the police and sheriff's reports; they had been humorously written and for the most part recounted teenage pranks and burglaries whose perpetrators were hilariously naive and inept. But in recent years those columns had become dry and factual; now they spoke of armed robberies and a sharp increase in drug use and domestic violence—all, she supposed, symptomatic of what was happening in small towns the world over. In this part of Northern California the rate of change was further aggravated by the urban/suburban sprawl from the San Francisco Bay Area, and the attendant problems were more severe because they had not been prepared for. Joanna, who had moved here to escape just such pressures, found the news uniformly depressing; lately she'd confined her reading to the arts and entertainment section and the real estate ads—the latter as a purely academic exercise.

Now she watched Sally Jane approach the table, a plate of blueberry muffins in one hand, in the other a cup of coffee with a big Danish balanced on top. The reporter was a tall, skinny blond; her diet consisted of junk food, mainly eaten on the run. Doughnuts, Big Macs, candy bars, french fries, and tacos disappeared quickly into her wide clown's mouth, their calories to be transformed by her marvelous metabolism into an enormous energy whose expending would only make her more lean and muscular. Sometimes Joanna—who had trouble maintaining the 110 pounds that would permit her to squeeze into her jeans—hated Sally Jane for that metabolic ability and seeming lack of need for fresh fruit and vegetables. Secretly she wished the reporter would come down with scurvy, or at very least wake up on her fortieth birthday to find she'd gained 200 pounds.

Joanna had met Sally Jane through her best friend Mary Bennett, who owned a quilt shop near the plaza. They had hit it off immediately, discovering a mutual interest in art, and periodically made forays to galleries and museums throughout the area. More than that, however, Sally Jane had become Joanna's primary source of information on Sonoma happenings and people.

For the four years Joanna had lived in the town, she'd felt very much the outsider. Her roots were in the city, her business was there; even Mary was a former advertising copywriter from San Francisco. E.J. had worked as a bartender at a restaurant on the plaza and made friends easily, but they were mainly of his own generation. Sally Jane, on the other hand, was a native of the valley—the first with whom Joanna had become intimate. With her help, she was gradually coming to feel a part of things in her chosen home.

This morning her purpose in consulting with Sally Jane was more serious than merely gathering gossip, however. It was, in fact, deadly serious.

Sally Jane set her food down and pulled up a chair. "Sorry I'm late," she said. "Big accident up near Kenwood. Guess who got stuck covering it." She took a sip of coffee and was about to pick up her Danish when she looked closely at Joanna and frowned. "What's the matter with you—hung over?"

Sally Jane had what Joanna's mother had called a "rubber face": In spite of her thirty-nine years, her skin was elastic and smooth, her features large and exceptionally mobile. When she smiled she looked like Punch, the idiotically happy puppet; when she frowned she resembled Punch's shrewish wife Judy. Now the frown deepened to a scowl as she began to suspect there might be more wrong with Joanna than a simple hangover.

Quickly Joanna said, "Yes, sort of. Nick Alexander came up for dinner last night, and we fixed Chinese. You know how that goes—chop a little, drink a little, stir-fry something, drink some more..."

Sally Jane nodded, biting into the Danish. From the dreamy look that came into her eyes, Joanna guessed she was envisioning dozens of little cardboard cartons filled with Chinese takeout. "You managed to get up and call me before seven, though," she said.

"I couldn't sleep." It was the truth; she'd been awake since four-thirty.

"Tough luck. So what's up?"

Now came the tricky part—extracting information from Sally Jane without revealing the actual reason she wanted it. Joanna needed to get a line on Parducci, determine if he had reason to be here in the valley other than taking his revenge on her. It had been her experience with the thief turned broker that he did not go out of his way to take care of personal business. If he had a client in the area or was seeking to arrange a theft there, it would certainly occur to him to settle his score with her at the same time. But it was unlikely that a man wanted by Interpol for two murders would risk entering the United States under false documentation simply for that purpose. The stakes would need to be significantly higher.

Of course, she thought suddenly, Parducci was a very changed man from the young thief whom she had known intimately many years before. He had not been a killer then. Nor had he been insane....

Joanna shivered.

"You sure you're not coming down with something?" Sally Jane asked.

For an instant she was tempted to tell her friend everything, enlist her aid. But just as she'd become conditioned to keeping secrets, she'd also developed a strong independent bent; many a friend, both male and female, had accused her of being too intent on handling everything herself, accepting help from no quarter. This, she knew, was a valid criticism, but there was not much she could do to change. And besides, the problem with Parducci was deeply personal. Foolish or not, she wanted to deal with it on her own terms—and alone.

"I'm okay," she said. "Sally Jane, do you remember how I intended to open a gallery when I moved up here?"

"Yeah. Bad idea. Shitload of galleries already." Sally Jane finished the Danish and offered Joanna a muffin.

She waved it away, her nervous stomach lurching. "I know that, but I'm wondering—there's a lot of money in the valley. There must be quite a few collectors."

"Sure, but that type goes to the city, New York, even Europe to buy."

"Who?"

"Who collects? You do. Me, on a more modest scale."

"I'm serious, Sally Jane."

"Okay. The Andrettis—wine money, but out of the business now. Old man Donatello might have an interest, but it'd be narrow. The Williamses, you know them. Ella DeVries. There's a couple of writers—I can't remember their names. Up the valley you've got some Hollywood types, but their taste sucks. That's about it."

"Have you ever heard any talk about people whose collecting interests might be bent?"

Sally Jane's eyes narrowed. While in her cups one night the previous fall, Joanna had told her she'd spent years trying to entrap a broker who dealt in Dutch and Flemish works. "You on to that guy again?"

"I told you—he's dead."

"Someone else, then?"

"Well, Nick *was* here last night." Let Sally Jane believe her inquiries were related to a job for SSI.

"Mmm." The reporter dabbed at the crumbs on her plate with her index finger.

Joanna tried a different tack. "What about upcoming shows or auctions at the local galleries? Have you heard of anything unusual happening there?"

"Shit, no. Want to hear what's in the entertainment section this week?" Sally Jane rummaged in her overstuffed handbag and extracted one of her notebooks. "That restaurant out on West Napa Street is changing hands for the fortieth time. New movie at the Sebastiani got a bad review. Wine auction Friday night—fundraiser, to try to make up the Donatello campaign's deficit. High school's putting on *Who's Afraid of Virginia Woolf*—imagine kids in those roles! Charlie and the Mad Dogs open at the Carbaret Sauvignon Saturday. You want me to go on?"

"Forget it." She was silent for a moment, staring into her coffee cup.

"Sure you won't tell me what's going on?"

"It's confidential business."

Now Sally Jane was silent. When she spoke again she pitched her voice lower. "Listen, I know of somebody who might be able to help you. You know the old Madrone Springs Resort?"

"Near Boyes, northwest of Highway Twelve?"

"Yeah. Guy's name is Davis Deane. Owns it. Lives in one of those broken-down cabins. Go see him, but after dark—he's only getting up then. Take a couple of bottles—cheap stuff, red, will do it."

"Who is he?"

"Old man who used to be somebody in the valley, until...well, just go talk to him."

"How do you know him?"

"Tried to interview him a couple of times. Human interest stuff, but he wouldn't give me anything I could use. Just drank up my wine and talked a lot about nothing. Maybe you'll have more luck."

"Tell me—"

Sally Jane glanced at her watch. "Got to go. Call me at the office later, I'll give you more details."

"Where are you off to in such a hurry?"

The reporter's wide mouth stretched into a smirk. "Interview with the proprietor of the new Hug Shop."

"The what?"

"You heard me. Teddy bears. Cups with hearts on 'em. Pillows with cutesy mottoes. Nauseating I-love-you shit."

"Good God."

"What can I tell you? It's a living." She stood, then paused beside the table. "That's why your gallery was a bad idea. This place is turning into a tourist trap; you'd probably have had to go the Hug Shop route, and you've got too many principles for that. What I really admire about you, Jo—you never compromise."

After Sally Jane left, Joanna sat at the table for a long time, contemplating the traffic on East Napa Street. It all went to show, she thought, how little her friend understood her. Because she *did* compromise.

Sometimes it seemed that compromise was all she'd ever done....

STOLEN
Subject: Theft of a Painting
Date of Theft: October 1987
Country: U.S.A.
An 18.9 cm × 28.4 cm oil-on-panel painting entitled Scene from a Graveyard by Flemish landscaper Jacob van Ruisdael (1628?–82), signed RUISDAEL in the lower left hand corner, and worth $53,790 American

dollars, was stolen from the Bass Museum of Art, Miami Beach, Florida, U.S.A. on October 17 1987.

It depicts a graveyard, showing several headstones in the foreground, dark green trees in the background on the left, and a stone church in the background on the right, partially obscured by purple and grayish clouds. See also accompanying photograph.

PLEASE INFORM GALLERIES, SALESROOMS, ANTIQUE DEALERS, PAWNBROKERS, MUSEUMS, CUSTOMS AUTHORITIES.

Joanna looked up from the Interpol bulletin and sighed. She was seated on the floor of her upstairs study, the door closed in case E.J. should return and take her unaware. Around her were spread dozens of weekly bulletins of stolen objects, monthly sheets listing the twelve most wanted works of art, and the corresponding photographs, issued by Interpol's art-theft squad. She had already set aside two large stacks of circulars from various foreign, federal, and local law enforcement agencies, as well as others from private organizations. Together they represented nearly a year's worth of international thieving—over $100 million dollars in value.

For over a decade Joanna had regularly received bulletins from these sources. She routinely separated out those listing Dutch or Flemish works, then pored over them, looking for a pattern that would tell her about Antony Parducci's current activities. None had appeared until the previous spring; then she'd acted quickly, devising an elaborate plan of entrapment that had ended in disaster. During the past twelve months SSI's secretary had continued to forward the bulletins from the firm's San Francisco office. Joanna had merely filed the envelopes unopened, in the futile hope that by such an action she would eventually convince herself that Parducci was dead. But all the while she had felt the file box on the floor of the study's closet pulling at her like a magnet.

This afternoon she'd sorted through the bulletins, read the pertinent ones, and once again detected no pattern. None of the thefts of Dutch or Flemish art clustered geographically or chronologically; none of the stolen works bore any relationship to one another. Their individual values were not high enough to justify the necessary risk to a broker of Parducci's stature, and as a group they lacked any particular appeal to a collector.

In fact, while art thefts were up in volume—as they seemed to be every year—thefts of Dutch and Flemish works, as well as the Old Masters, were down. Enthusiasm seemed to be running high for Impressionist and Post-Impressionist paintings, and Joanna attributed this trend to the record prices such works were bringing at auction these days. It had all started the previous year when the successful bid at Christie's of London for Vincent Van Gogh's *Sunflowers* had stood at $39.9 million. Less than eight months later Sotheby's in New York had sold the same artist's *Irises* for $49 million. And since then inflation had run rampant in the art world.

Joanna was vociferously opposed to such enormous private sales: They artificially drove up all prices, and placed the best paintings in the hands of a moneyed elite, denying the public the opportunity to view them. Until a few years ago, it had been reasonably certain that such works would eventually make their way to museums as donations or bequests, but—at least in the United States—recent changes in the tax laws had made such gifts costly and unfeasible. When collections were broken up now, the paintings usually were returned to the auction block, where their prices were further inflated, and then placed in other private collections.

Joanna also recognized a potentially dangerous aspect of the trend: While the identities of the successful bidders were usually kept secret, speculation always centered on the Japanese. They had, everyone said, vast discretionary income, both as a nation and as individuals. There was a great deal of talk at openings and benefits (when only occidentals were present) about how the Japanese viewed artworks as merely another marketable commodity akin to gold, silver, or pork bellies. And there was a certain amount of supercilious amusement over the well-known Japanese fondness for pictures of flowers. Every time Joanna heard such a conversation, she couldn't help but wonder if this wasn't a new, insidious form of racism.

After a moment she stretched and began crawling around, gathering the bulletins and replacing them in the file box. The afternoon had slipped by without her noticing the time; dusk had fallen and her stomach growled noisily. She would grab a quick sandwich, then stop off at the liquor store for a couple of bottles of cheap red en route to visit Davis Deane at the Madrone Springs Resort. But first she'd try to call Sally Jane again.

She put the lid on the file box and went to the phone that sat on David's old rolltop desk. As earlier, the reporter wasn't in the office, had been out on a story since two. Joanna tried her home number on the off chance she might have returned there, but got only the machine. Irritated, she hung up on it. It would serve her friend right for not being in the proper place when needed.

Joanna really didn't want to drop in on Deane without knowing more about him. Sally Jane had said she had once tried to get a story out of the old man, but failed. If such an expert interviewer couldn't extract information from him, it was doubtful Joanna could, either. And certainly not without knowing what sort of questions to ask.

E.J.'s motorcycle sounded in the drive below. Joanna shut off the light and hurried out of the study, paranoically

afraid that her mere presence there might tell him she'd once
again been perusing her files. She'd skip the sandwich, she
decided, and catch a burger (á la Sally Jane) at McDonald's
on the way. If E.J. asked where she was going, she'd say to
an exercise class at the community center. That was one
thing he wouldn't dream of asking to tag along to.

FOUR

CALIFORNIA HIGHWAY 12 runs north from Sonoma to the city of Santa Rosa, some eighteen miles distant. It is bordered by wooded mountains and prime grape-growing acreage, plus a number of little unincorporated communities—Boyes Hot Springs, Fetters Hot Springs, Agua Caliente—which are mere clusters of houses and stores whose colorful past has faded to a dingy present.

In their heyday, Fetters, Boyes, and Agua Caliente were a mecca for devotees of mineral baths, who traveled by rail from the Bay Area to take the waters, as well as to enjoy vaudeville, movies, concerts, and dances. Prohibition ushered in a gaudier era: The often sultry valley nights rang with the sounds of jazz, cocktail-hour laughter, and drunken shouts from the speakeasies and whorehouses. But in the years following Repeal, the popularity of the spas declined and life in the little towns became more sedate. One last colorful establishment—Juanita's Gallery, a Fetters restaurant whose bawdy, muumuu-clad owner was alleged to be a former madam—burned to the ground in the 1970s.

Today the string of towns consists of shabby businesses and generally substandard housing; the sultry nights echo with the sounds of bar brawls. Up until a few years ago the state frequently released ex-convicts to the area because of the plentiful supply of "affordable" housing—much of it run-down summer cottages left over from the glory days. Agua Caliente swimming pool is still in operation, and some reasonably expensive tracts have sprung up, but by and large the only sign of real prosperity is the Sonoma Mission Inn and Spa—a pink pile of pseudo-Spanish stucco that caters

to the nouveau riche. Within a stone's throw of its landmark water tower more drug deals are said to be transacted
than in any other part of the county.

At around seven-thirty that evening Joanna drove her Fiat
past the trailer parks and thrift shops, the taverns and legal
poker parlors. Once in open country, she increased her
speed, eyes alert for Madrone Springs Road. The turnoff
came up so fast that she had to brake sharply. Behind her,
a VW beeped indignantly.

The potholed pavement angled away from the highway
toward the dark hills to the west. Joanna switched her
headlights onto high beam and straddled the center of the
road, which crumbled away at both edges into an overgrown drainage ditch. To the right was a vineyard, staked
grapevines marching in regular patterns across it. To the left
the land was heavily wooded; beyond the trees she could see
lights—faint, the way they appear before full dark sets in.

Joanna was familiar with the road, and with Madrone
Springs Resort, as were most local residents who enjoyed
long Sunday drives in the countryside. The mouldering resort was a county landmark, often featured in arty photographs, and quite a legend had grown up around it. The
story was that it had been *the* spa in the valley before Prohibition; silent-movie stars and even royalty were said to
have stayed there. After the Volstead Act, an eccentric mil-
lionaire had set up his mistress—a White Russian known
only as Natalia—there. When he abandoned her for another woman, Natalia became the county's most notorious
madam. In 1939 she suddenly disappeared, leaving behind
a fortune in jewels and cash, and for a while rumors circu-
lated: that she had returned to Russia; fled to Nazi Ger-
many; been murdered by Soviet agents; gone underground
as a spy for the Japanese. Then, as the war effort geared up,
interest in Natalia dropped off and she was forgotten.

After that point the story of Madrone Springs Resort became vague, possibly because most of it had only been fic-

tion to begin with. The buildings remained—on a rise above a ravine, surrounded by a grove of oak trees, scoured a soft gray by the elements. The three-story hotel slumped to one side; under its portico stood a rusted-out automobile. The cottages that were scattered in the grove behind the main building—some dozen of them—sagged on their crumbling foundations.

No one knew much about the resort today. It was said there was a hot-spring-fed swimming pool full of debris in the courtyard of the boarded-up hotel. It was said there were steps leading down into the ravine, where the ruins of a dance pavilion stood beside the creek. It was periodically rumored that developers had bought the property and planned to restore it. And it was also rumored that on warm windy nights the ghost of Natalia walked from cabin to cabin....

In fact, Joanna thought now, the only concrete thing she had ever heard about Madrone Springs Resort was what Sally Jane had told her this morning: that a man named Davis Deane owned it and lived in one of the cabins. A man who might have information that would help her.

She came to a fork in the road and slowed, eyes straining against the darkness. The resort was ahead and to her right, the hotel looming charcoal gray before a backdrop of black trees. Through them, to the left, a faint light showed.

Joanna pulled her car into a graveled area in front of the hotel, next to an antiquated pickup. Her headlights revealed high windows that had been boarded up and reinforced with a crisscross of planks. The massive double doors were chained and padlocked. The derelict car under the portico looked to be a sixties-vintage sedan; it had no windows or wheels, and the right front door was missing; inside the upholstery had rotted away, leaving only a metal seat frame.

She was about to turn the Fiat's engine off when she saw a second light in the trees to the left of the building. It bobbed up and down, disappeared and reappeared, as if someone was weaving through them. Joanna waited, hand on the ignition.

The man who emerged from the grove was clearly visible in the bright beam from his lantern: gray haired, with a deeply furrowed face and heavily stubbled jowls; lean and stooped, but moving in a gait that showed he was not frail; dressed in wrinkled and patched workclothes; carrying a shotgun.

Joanna studied the man. He held the shotgun easily, like a hunter walking through the woods or a foot soldier on a routine patrol. He stopped at the edge of the gravel, peered at her car, and waited. His stance was wary, but not aggressive.

Joanna shut off the engine and got out of the Fiat, the liquor store sack in her arms.

The man neither moved nor spoke.

"Mr. Deane?" she called. "Davis Deane?"

"You've found him." Deane's voice was hoarse and cracked with age.

"Sally Jane Lane sent me, Mr. Deane. The reporter from the Sonoma paper? She spoke with you once—"

"I remember her."

"She said you might help me with—" With what? She didn't even know what to ask him, for God's sake! "I need to talk with you, Mr. Deane. I've brought some wine." She held out the bag in front of her.

Deane's eyes moved to it, then back to her face. "The Lane woman tell you to do that, too?"

"She mentioned that you like red."

His lips twitched in the beginning of a smile. "Bourbon's my drink, but wine'll do. Woman got me pretty damn drunk the night she came by with her cheap burgundy. I'll talk to you, but first let me ask you this: Are you in the real estate business?"

"No."

"You sure?"

"Absolutely."

"What did you say your name was?"

"I didn't. Joanna Stark."

"Stark." He paused. "Used to be Starks out on Old Winery Road, near the Haraszthy place."

The Haraszthy place was Buena Vista Winery, but Joanna had never heard it called after the family who had founded it many years ago. Davis Deane must be older than he looked. "There're still Starks there," she said. "I inherited the house five years ago."

"Young Joseph's gone?"

Joseph was the name of the uncle who had left the house to David. "Yes."

Deane nodded, not looking particularly surprised or saddened. "All right, girl, you may as well come ahead. But watch your step—the ground's tunneled by gophers. For all I know, one of those holes is the front door to hell."

She approached him, the sack cradled against her. Deane raised the lantern and scrutinized her face. "You don't look like a Stark," he said. His breath reeked of whiskey.

"I married into the family."

"Where's your husband, that he's letting you come out here alone like this?"

"He died four years ago." As she spoke, Joanna felt a tightening in her breast—not the wrenching pain she used to feel, but a twinge nonetheless. She suspected it would always happen when she mentioned David's death, and she took an odd sort of comfort from that.

Deane grunted, a brusque expression of sympathy. Then he turned and led her silently through the grove. The darkness was thick outside the yellowish circle from the lantern; birds rustled about in the branches above them. Ahead she could see the light she'd spied as she'd driven in. As they neared it she saw the faint outline of the cabin. The rush of the creek in the ravine below became audible, and she caught the scent of fresh bay laurel.

The cabin stood on the edge of the tangled underbrush that cascaded into the ravine: a rough board structure, perhaps two rooms, with a swaybacked roof and canted front porch. Through the window that was backlit by an oil lamp, Joanna caught sight of an antiquated iron wood stove and a sink with a hand pump.

The old man stepped onto the porch, leaned the shotgun against the wall next to the screen door, and set the lantern on an upended orange crate. There was a chair positioned on either side of the crate—metal, with curving tubular legs, formerly white but now scaled with rust. Joanna wondered if other people visited Deane, to sit with him on this sloping porch and talk and drink, or if the arrangement of chairs was merely the expression of a forlorn hope.

He turned to her and reached for the sack. "Wait here, we'll talk outside," he said, then went through the screen door.

She looked at the chairs, trying to judge which one Deane favored. A butt-filled ashtray on the right half of the crate told her, so she sat in the other. From the cabin came clinking and splashing sounds: Deane washing glasses. In a moment he emerged, carrying one of the wine bottles and a pair of tumblers. He set them down, poured both full to the brim, and raised his.

"To your health."

"And yours." The wine was heavy and acidic.

Deane downed almost the entire glass and poured it full again before he sat. "You've saved me a trip into Boyes," he said. "I'd planned to spend my evening at Rosa's Tavern. Do you know that fine establishment?" His tone was faintly self-mocking.

Joanna nodded. Rosa's Tavern often figured prominently in the paper's sheriff's reports.

"It's not as bad as they say." Deane fished a cigarette out of his shirt pocket and lit it. "They've got a wide-screen TV that's easy on my eyes, and Rosa lets me run a tab. I'm too old for the studs to pick fights with, and I don't carry much money so nobody's tried to roll me."

The level of wine in Deane's glass had already fallen. He topped it off again and glanced at Joanna's. "Not much of a drinker, are you?"

"Not much," she lied.

"Starks never were, so you married into the right family. Old Joseph—he was as tight-assed as they come. Young Joseph was just too damned cheap. How was your husband related to them?"

"A nephew, from the San Francisco branch of the family."

"And what's this young fellow who just bought the winery—Elliot J. Stark—to you?"

"My son."

"He's got himself a fine piece of land there, if he knows what to do with it."

"You're familiar with the winery, then?"

"Familiar with it? Girl, I used to own it!"

That surprised her; the people E.J. had bought from were called Gianelli.

Seeing her bewilderment, Deane said, "That was a long time ago. I used to own a lot of land in this valley. Vineyards, dairyland, too. Lived in Sonoma all my life. That big house on East Napa Street—the white one with the high box hedge around it?"

"The Deane house. Of course." On Sonoma's list of homes with a history it ranked right up there. She was surprised she hadn't made the connection.

"Had it built myself in the nineteen-twenties," the old man said, nodding in remembered satisfaction. "Could have lived elsewhere, had property all up and down the valley, even in Santa Rosa. But the wife had her garden club, her church societies, and the boy liked being near his play-mates."

"You have a son?"

"Had."

"And your wife?"

"She's gone, too."

He was closing up on her. She cast about for a subject that would set him talking again. In order to find out what helpful information he might possess, she needed to know more about Davis Deane. Besides, she liked the old man, for some indefinable reason felt a strong positive connection to him. "Mr. Deane," she said, "before you allowed me to come onto your property, you asked if I was in real estate. Why?"

"Because I won't have one of the goddamned vultures on the place. They're after my land."

"They want to restore the resort?"

"Some of 'em. Others want to bulldoze it, build condos or tracts. That's not going to happen—this place is all I've got left." Deane tossed back the rest of his wine and looked at her half-full glass. "Drink up, girl. I'll get us the other bottle."

When he went inside, Joanna poured most of her wine into the shrubbery at the far side of the porch. Deane came back out, refilled both glasses, and settled into his chair. It gave a muted squeak, as if it were too old and worn out to protest much.

"Like I was saying," he continued, "nobody's going to get me to sell. I lost the vineyards, the dairyland. Lost the house in town, the ranch near Glen Ellen, the property in Santa Rosa. The wife and the boy—they're gone, too. This land is the last thing in this world that means anything to me besides the bottle; it's where I'll stay as long as I'm above-ground."

He gave her a sly sidelong glance and added, "And that'll be a goddamned long time, too. I'm eighty-eight. Was born at the turn of the century, and I plan to be here to usher in the new one."

"What happened that you lost everything?"

Deane either didn't hear her or chose not to. "I've seen the changes in this valley," he said. "I've seen what men can do to something clean and beautiful. Women, too. Greed. Selfishness. I've holed up in this cabin for damned near twenty-five years, never go anyplace except Rosa's, a couple of the other bars. But I'll tell you, it's better than all their fancy dinner parties and benefits. Better, and more honest."

Joanna waited, but the old man didn't go on. After a moment he took out another cigarette. His motions were sure and measured; the quantity of wine he'd drunk—plus whatever he'd had before she arrived—had not slurred his speech. She sensed he was one of those controlled alcoholics who are able to blot out whatever makes them drink by maintaining an even, continuous high.

After he got the cigarette going, Deane spoke again. "You said you needed some help."

"Yes. I don't know how to put this—"

"Just spit it out, girl."

"All right. Sally Jane Lane sent me to you...I guess because of all you know about the valley. You seem to know a lot about its past, but also about its present. You knew about my son buying the winery, for instance."

Deane smiled faintly. "The taverns of Boyes aren't so far removed from the fine homes of Sonoma as you might think. In fact, you're more apt to get the true story of what goes on by keeping your ears open at the bar."

"Well...there's a man who's come to the valley who wants to harm me. I need to find out where he is, what he's planning."

Deane was silent. After a moment he said, "The man have a name?"

"Antony Parducci."

"Never known of any Parduccis around here."

"He's not from here; he's an Italian national and has spent most of his life in Europe. He's an art thief."

She wasn't sure, but she thought Deane stiffened slightly. After a moment he said, "Why're you afraid of this Parducci? You have something he wants to steal?"

"He's already stolen a painting from me, yesterday. But I think he also intends to kill me."

Slowly Deane turned his head toward her. His eyes were narrowed, his lips pulled into a rigid line. "Why would he want to do that?"

". . . I've kept him from getting his hands on some things he wanted. We . . . go back a long way."

"How long?"

"About the same amount of time you've been living here at the resort."

Deane looked away, his eyes fixed on some point in the surrounding darkness. "You know," he said, "I knew the Starks pretty well. Didn't like them much, but they were townspeople. Back then you stood by your townspeople; they were like family. I guess that makes you and me more or less related, doesn't it?"

"I guess."

"Being related, I wish I could help you. But I never heard of this Parducci, this art thief. The only—" And then he was silent, sitting still as stone.

"Mr. Deane?"

Another head shake—this time the way a dog shakes off water. After a moment he said, "You let me think on this, girl. There might be an answer."

"Can't you give me some idea—"

"No. Let me think on it."

"It's urgent—"

"Girl, I've lived a long time. Believe me, a day or two won't matter."

"When can we talk again?"

"Tomorrow night. Come the same time." Deane gave her another of his sidelong glances; this time his self-mockery was open. "Bring a couple more bottles—but this time make it bourbon."

FIVE

ON HER WAY home Joanna drove slowly, trying to understand why she felt such a strong bond to Davis Deane. His claim that they were more or less related was correct, but she sensed that had less to do with their mutual connection to the Stark family than it did with their being kindred spirits. The old man had been badly hurt by life but had survived, slightly maimed; so had Joanna. Deane's alcoholism was the equivalent of her constant fear—afflictions they lived with and attempted to keep under control. That was why she'd felt comfortable with him from the first. She felt as if she'd known him for a long, long time....

And then she remembered another old man—one of David's San Francisco friends who had been kind to her at a time when few other people even cared to try. They'd also had an instant rapport; like Deane, he'd addressed her as "girl" in an affectionate and nonchauvinistic way. That man was dead now: because of his own mistakes, to be sure, but indirectly because of Parducci. Remembering, she felt a strong panic, as if history might repeat itself. She had a strong unreasonable urge to turn the car around and rush back to Madrone Springs Resort to make sure Deane was all right.

When she pulled into her own driveway the lights were on both in the living room and the upstairs study; the surge of adrenaline that went through her upon seeing them was almost dizzying. She told herself it was unlikely that Parducci would visit her house again, much less go about turning on lights. But earlier E.J. had said he planned to stop in to see his former coworkers at Mario's tonight, and there was no one else . . .

Then she saw her son's motorcycle and realized he hadn't gone out after all. The pounding of her heart lessened measurably.

She parked her car at the top of the drive and hurried inside, annoyance prickling when she found that E.J. hadn't locked the door. After securing it, she glanced into the living room, then went up to the study. Her son sat at the rolltop desk, his back to the door; when she entered he swiveled around and glared accusingly at her. She looked down at the floor, saw the file box where she'd left it earlier. Stupid mistake—she'd meant to put it back in the closet.

E.J. said, "So you're at it again."

Joanna instinctively employed an evasionary tactic her own mother had used—and one she herself hated. "What are you doing in here?"

"I didn't realize the study was off limits to me. If you want to know, I found that printout that Nick brought you on the kitchen counter with Herman draped over it. I dragged it up here so it wouldn't get damaged." He paused. "And then I found those files."

For a moment she was tempted to pretend innocence, to say she'd merely been cleaning the closet and had forgotten to put the box back. But from the expression on his face she could tell he'd looked inside and seen that the bulletins had been removed from their envelopes and sorted.

"Why, Jo?" E.J. said. "You can't go on trying to keep tabs on a dead man."

She crossed to the window and looked out across the front lawn. The moon, near full, hung high above the persimmon tree; its rays silvered the eucalyptus grove across the road.

What she had here, she thought, was a critical moment of choice. Tell him the truth, and risk the consequences.

Withhold it, and watch their always precariously balanced relationship fall apart.

"He's not dead," she said.

E.J. sighed. "Jo, we've been over and over this—"

"He's not dead!"

E.J. caught his breath. And waited.

"Come with me," she said. "I have to show you something." She led him downstairs and pointed to the empty hook on the wall in the hallway.

"Oh, Jo, why did you take it down? *Dark Star* was there to remind you never to concoct any more crazy schemes like last year in England!"

"Someone took it down for me." She went to the hall chair and got the matchbook from where she'd hidden it in the seat compartment. "Here, look at this."

At first he merely seemed puzzled, but when he read the hotel name his lips twitched. "Where did you get it?"

"It was left on the burl table at the same time *Dark Star* was taken. As a calling card."

E.J. stepped through the archway and stared at the burl, as if it could tell him who had put the matchbook there. After a moment he said, "It didn't have to be Parducci, you know."

"Who else?"

"…Maybe Rafferty's back. He's got to be pissed at you; you sent him away."

Rafferty was her former lover, who had badly betrayed her. "No," she said, "Steve's not like that. Whatever his other faults, he doesn't play childish games."

"Well, who else knows what really went on over there?"

"No one."

E.J. shook his head in stubborn denial. He went farther into the living room, looked down at the matchbook in his hand, and flung it at the fireplace. It bounced off the mantel and landed on the rug.

"Dammit, Jo!" he exclaimed. "When did this happen?"

"Yesterday afternoon, while I was up at your winery."

"Why didn't you tell me right away?"

She shrugged, not looking at him.

But E.J. guessed the unspoken reply. He flushed and turned away from her, fists clenched, fighting for control. After a moment he said in a thick voice, "You still don't trust me, do you?"

"It has nothing to do with trust."

"What, then?"

"I wanted to protect you. I planned to tell you once I was sure what was going on. But until then I didn't see the need—"

"Don't you realize how sick I am of being protected?"

"I think I probably do. But it's an old habit—"

"I'll say it is!" He whirled, his face congested with anger. "You protected me from Parducci when I was a baby. Okay, I know you had to do that, and I'm grateful. But then when you married David you 'protected' me by letting me go on thinking I was his natural son and Eleanor my natural mother. And for the longest time after I suspected you and David had been having an affair before Eleanor died, long after I was old enough to understand, you denied that, too. Was that 'protecting' me, Jo? Or was it really protecting you?"

"E.J., I thought this was all settled between us—"

"So did I. Maybe it's not. For all I know there're more secrets lurking in the wings."

"What's that supposed to mean?"

"All right—it was a cheap shot. But you're still withholding things from me because you think I can't handle them. Jo, I'm twenty-three years old. I've been more or less on my own since I graduated from high school. I've bummed around the country, held down jobs when I needed to, hardly touched the money David left me until I sank it into the winery. I pay my way; I'm giving you a fair percentage of the business for your investment. Sure, I smoke some dope, and I can't seem to settle down with one woman. But I happen to think I've got my head screwed on pretty well and my priorities pretty straight. Why do you have to persist in the notion that I'm a little boy?''

She laced her fingers together in front of her, gripping so tightly that they hurt. "I don't—"

"You *do*. Maybe not consciously, but your actions show it. You're *tolerant* about the dope. You're *amused* by my troubles with women. You think I'll *outgrow* the motorcycle and wearing a beard and liking to go off with my backpack and hitch around the countryside. Well, maybe I will—but in the meantime do you have to be so damned condescending toward me?''

"I don't feel condescending. In fact, I admire your self-sufficiency. You have a confidence and a freedom of spirit that I used to, but lost. And the only times I ever shield you any more are in matters relating to Parducci—"

"Parducci! Jesus Christ, I wish I'd never heard the name! Never laid eyes on the son of a bitch. Here I thought he was dead—was happy about it, for God's sake—and now he's trying to barge back into our lives—"

"E.J., it's more than that. I think he means to kill me."

Her son froze. He stared at her for a moment, his electric blue eyes—the only feature he had inherited from Parducci—going hard and flat. "Just let him try. Let the bastard try, and I'll kill him first.''

"He's your father—"

"Fatherhood means more than just accidentally donating your sperm. He's not my father, never has been. Goddammit, why didn't he just stay dead?''

He started for the door, brushing roughly past her. "Where are you going?'' she demanded.

He fumbled with the double lock and chain. "Out of here—if I can get this fucking door open!''

"Don't do—"

He wrenched the chain free, faced her. "Don't do anything rash? Is that what you're about to say? I wouldn't worry. If someone of your talents has trouble finding the bastard, I sure as hell wouldn't have any luck, either. But let him come near you or me, just one time—"

As he left he closed the door with a deliberate firmness that was more frightening than if he'd slammed it so hard the windows rattled.

THE HOURS PASSED slowly. E.J. didn't return. Joanna attempted to read until midnight, then put her book aside and sat on the couch in the dark, waiting. And contemplating a subject she would sooner have left alone—but knew she'd better face up to.

A number of the things E.J. had said to her had seemed unfair and wounded her deeply, but she was self-aware enough to recognize a kernel of truth in them. And that forced her to reexamine her attitude toward him; what she discovered wasn't particularly pleasant.

Underneath all her protectiveness, her amusement at his youthful foibles, her tolerance—well, maybe it *was* condescension—underneath all that lurked a resentment. Resentment, because his birth had robbed her forever of the freedom she'd run away from home at nineteen to seek.

At twenty she'd been a mother, and totally disillusioned. At twenty-one she'd commenced years of wandering through Europe, North Africa, Asia—any place to get away from Parducci and keep him from finding where the son he sought to claim really was. She'd eventually felt it was safe to go to San Francisco, had taken up residence in a shabby apartment, gotten a low-paying job as a burglar alarm installer—all so she could be near E.J. if he needed her.

It was pure happenstance that Nick Alexander had recognized her talent and intelligence and allowed her to help him transform SSI from a small installation firm to a full-

service security operation. It was sheer luck that David—
who had been her father's best friend in law school—had
literally stumbled over her while she was installing an alarm
at one of his clients' galleries; had begun arranging for her
to see her son; had fallen in love with her.

And still E.J.'s welfare had come first: David didn't leave
his cold and emotionally troubled wife for Joanna; for his
adoptive son's sake he kept up the appearance of a marriage until Eleanor died. And while Joanna was the one to
suggest they not tell E.J. about his parentage, that was only
because she knew David wanted it that way. "For the boy's
well-being" she'd suffered the scorn of her husband's society friends; E.J.'s anger at what she'd done to the woman he
thought was his mother; the rage of David's relatives when
they discovered he'd left "that woman" nearly his entire
fortune. For her son's sake she'd kept secrets, denied herself, risked her own happiness.

She'd had no idea until now how much she resented it.
And him.

It was an emotion she would have to face and attempt to
exorcise—or it would poison the rest of their lives.

Too much introspection eventually wore her out. She fell
asleep, woke fitfully, slept again. When the phone rang it
was still dark. She twisted on the couch and mumbled,
"E.J.?"

The phone rang again. She reached for it, her arm entan-
gled in the blanket that she'd wrapped around her. The receiver slipped from her fingers and fell onto the end table.
She struggled to a sitting position and snatched it up. When
she spoke into it Sally Jane said, "Christ, what are you
doing—using the phone as a bowling ball?"

"Sorry. I was asleep. What time is it?"

"Five in the morning. I'm at Sonoma Valley Hospital—"

"E.J.?" She started to get off the couch.

"What? Listen, are you awake yet?"

"Now I am."

"Good. There's been another accident on the highway, this one down south near Schellville. Must have been the rain—"

"Rain?" She glanced at the window, saw only darkness.

"Storm blew in during the night. Roads're slicker than hell. I came here to see if I could find out about the crash victims. While I was waiting they brought Davis Deane in."

With a twinge of anxiety Joanna remembered her concern for the old man's safety. "What happened?"

"Ran his pickup off Highway Twelve between his place and Boyes last night. Was out there in the ditch until the sheriff's patrol spotted him a little after four. Doesn't look good for him—broken ribs, internal injuries, suffering from exposure. They just took him into surgery."

"My God. Was he drunk?"

"Don't know. Usually is. I take it you went up to talk to him."

"Yes. Why?"

"He was conscious when they brought him in. Recognized me. Gave me a message for you. You're to look in his papers—something there that might help you. And you're to do something about the vineyard at Marmande; if he doesn't make it, his great-granddaughter's to have it. He trusts you to take care of that, seeing as how you're more or less related. What does that mean? *Is* Deane a relative of yours?"

"No, we're just brand new friends." Tears stung her eyes.

"Well, what about this vineyard? Marmande. Where's that?"

"I don't know. I don't even know where his papers are."

Sally Jane was silent. "Well, one thing, Jo," she said, lowering her voice, "I think you better get up to his place and look for them right away. While Deane's still alive you're just doing a favor for a friend. If he dies you don't know how his next of kin—there's only the great-granddaughter—might feel about you going onto the property.''

''Right. I'll call you later.'' She hung up the receiver and headed for the door. If Deane had thought the message urgent enough to pass along from what might be his deathbed, she'd better go quickly.

SIX

DAWN WAS BREAKING as she drove up the valley. Its first rays backlit the swollen purple gray clouds that lowered over the hills to the east. The rain had diminished to a drizzle that refracted the lights of the other cars she encountered; the Fiat's own headlights made bright smears on the dark slick pavement. The air smelled fresh and clean—too full of promise for a morning when a newfound friend might be dying.

Although her eyes were intent on the road and her reflexes ready for an emergency, Joanna's thoughts were turned inward, her conscience waging a war with guilt.

If I hadn't taken the wine to Deane he might not have started drinking.

Nonsense—as Sally Jane said and Deane himself implied, he's usually drunk. He'd been drinking before you got there.

But he might have been relatively sober when he started for Rosa's Tavern.

He still would have been drunk going home.

And then she realized she was making an unfounded assumption about Deane having gone to Rosa's. She had no way of knowing where he'd been. She didn't even know in which direction he'd been traveling when his truck went in the ditch, much less what time it had happened. It was not light enough to scan the sides of the highway for physical evidence, so she contented herself with making a mental note to ask Sally Jane. By now the reporter would have learned details from the sheriff's department.

By the time she reached Madrone Springs Resort the
darkness was filtered and mist wrapped the hotel in a thick
blanket. She drove past and left her car a bit farther down
the road, then walked back, entering the grove from the side
opposite the building. The trees dripped copiously; her
boots squished on the ground and their high heels sank into
mud. From nearby came the overpowering smell that euca-
lypti give off after a rain.

The oil lamp still burned in the window of Deane's cabin,
its flame turned low. The empty wine bottle and two tumblers still sat on the crate between the rusted chairs. When
Joanna stepped onto the porch and opened the screen door,
there was a thumping noise behind her. She whirled in time
to see a yellow cat land on the ground and slink off into the
underbrush at the ravine's edge.

The inner door was unlocked, but dampness had swollen
it in its frame. She gave it a shove; it swung inward. The
small room beyond was a combination kitchen and living
area, furnished simply but comfortably; besides the iron
stove and sink with the hand pump that she'd earlier
glimpsed through the window, it contained a recliner chair,
Formica dinette set, brick-and-board bookcase, and thrift-
shop cabinet for dishes and canned goods. A rudimentary
bathroom opened off the room at the rear. Although she
had seen utility lines running onto the property, Joanna
guessed that Deane either had not had the service connected or chose not to use it much, in the interest of economy.

She went over to the oil lamp on the cabinet under the
window and turned up its flame. Except for the bookcase,
which covered the wall between the bathroom and a closed
door several feet to its right, there was nowhere that Deane
could have kept papers. She crossed and examined its contents: mostly paperbacks and used textbooks on a surprising array of subjects. Deane appeared to favor western and
spy fiction; Dickens and the poetry of T.S. Eliot; astron-

omy, economics, and anthropology; biographies of inventors and industrialists. There was an ancient *Encyclopedia Britannica* with several volumes missing; a moldy *Complete Works of Shakespeare*; a book on how to construct crossword puzzles, with several sheets of paper stuffed into it that showed someone had tried and given up. Apparently at one time Deane had thought to learn Chinese, but from the condition of the text it was doubtful anyone had ever gotten beyond page seventeen.

Even if she had never met him, the contents of this bookcase would have told her Deane was not your garden-variety drunk.

She tried the closed door next. It led into a bedroom, half the size of the living room, but better furnished. The old-fashioned bureau, nightstands, and bedstead had probably once graced the Deane House on East Napa Street; now their carvings and inlays were coated with grime. The tumbled quilts on the double bed might have been sewn by the wife who died; they too were soiled. On the bureau a set of tarnished silver brushes lined up on a tattered dresser scarf.

Joanna contemplated the room for a moment, saddened by the reminders of Deane's former life. Then she set to work systematically searching all of the drawers and possible hiding places. They yielded no papers. She returned to the front room and checked both it and the bathroom more thoroughly, but came up empty-handed. The cabin's construction was so simple that no cache could have escaped her notice. Finally she sat down on the recliner, discouraged.

Perhaps there weren't any papers, she thought. The old man had been in bad shape when he'd spoken to Sally Jane; he might just have been rambling. But that didn't seem right. If he'd been lucid enough to connect the reporter with her and reiterate his remark about the two of them being "more or less related," he'd certainly known what he was saying. Of course, Sally Jane could have gotten the message wrong; Deane might have said she should look in *the* papers, for instance. But that wasn't likely, either: Sally Jane was too good a reporter to get an essentially simple message garbled.

But what was this about a vineyard?

And where *were* the papers?

She remained in the chair, her gaze skipping restlessly about the room and finally settling on the window. The darkness had faded into the new day; through the misted trees she could see the old hotel, tinted purple by the distant storm clouds...

The old hotel.

The cabins would be easy to break into, presented an attractive target to vandals. Probably Deane had had trouble before; he'd met her last night with shotgun in hand. And although—for whatever reasons—he didn't care to live in the hotel, it was a fairly secure place where he could store anything of value.

She got up and moved toward the door, then hesitated. The hotel was boarded and padlocked; she'd need a key. Somewhere in the cabin she'd seen a set hanging on a hook...yes, over there under the top shelf of the cabinet, concealed from the casual glance yet near to hand. Joanna appropriated them and went out into the damp morning.

Silence hung heavy all around, but as she passed the thicket a racket of bird cries rose from the ravine. The clouds that had been piled high over the hills looked deflated now; they lay limply upon the peaks and drooped into the hollows. The sky above them glared white as the sun struggled to break through. The harsh light revealed the hotel's rotting facade in cruel detail.

Joanna paused behind the rusted-out sedan and looked up and down the road. Nothing moved, no vehicle was in sight. Still she hesitated, peering into the surrounding foliage and out over the neighboring vineyards. When she finally was certain no human eye could observe her actions, she went up to the tall double doors.

Only one of the keys on the ring looked as if it might work the padlock. She inserted it; it stuck. She jiggled it, gently, then harder. It turned and the padlock opened. She slipped it from the chain, unwound the chain from the latches, and tugged at the handle on the right side. The door opened soundlessly, as if its hinges had recently been oiled.

The interior was very dark, with only threads of daylight coming through cracks in the boards over the windows. Joanna fumbled in her purse and took out her small flashlight. She removed the padlock and chain from the other door handle and set them on the floor of the portico under the rusted-out car, then stepped inside and closed the door behind her.

The air was damp and smelled strongly of mold. Joanna brought the flashlight up and snapped it on. The thin beam showed a wide staircase straight ahead; to either side were archways. She tiptoed across the uncarpeted floor—knowing such stealth was not necessary but employing it anyway—to the one on her right; it opened on a large room that had been stripped of both furnishings and fixtures. There was a swinging door at its rear that led to a kitchen. Again, all equipment and fixtures had been removed, even the built-in cabinets—which, she judged, had probably been glass-fronted and attractive to antique dealers. A mousetrap—sprung, but containing no corpse or skeleton—lay on the floor in one corner.

She retraced her steps, crossed the lobby, and shone her light through the second archway. The room beyond it ran the entire length of the building. Drapes of some heavy dark material hung crooked at the boarded windows; above a stone fireplace was a poorly executed painting of a ballerina in the style of Degas, its pastel tones muddied by years of grime. At the rear of the room more heavy draperies were pulled the entire width of the wall; murky light seeped around them. Joanna went back there and yanked them aside.

Behind them were wide glass doors and windows of a style that had been popular in the 1920s—an improvement probably made during the hotel's gaudy days. They opened onto a covered courtyard, its roof composed of many small panes, like a greenhouse. The rumored swimming pool lay in the center of the court, drained and heaped with trash. Joanna turned the key that protruded from the doors' lock and stepped outside.

The courtyard's floor was blue and white tiles, many of them cracked or missing. Surprisingly, most of the panes of the greenhouse roof were intact. The stucco walls surrounding the court on the other three sides were eight feet high; a steep outward cant toward the top was designed to prevent intruders from climbing them. At the far end of the courtyard was a raised bandstand backed by fancy latticework.

Joanna looked about, her imagination carried away by what she saw. She pictured the courtyard as it might have been during the Jazz Age: tuxedo-clad musicians on the bandstand; men and women in cocktail-time attire sipping bootleg gin and dancing the Charleston or the Black Bottom. The parties would have become raucous and wild as the evenings wore on; many a formally dressed gentleman would have taken a plunge into the pool. The pool, which now was only a repository for odds and ends of wood, broken crockery and utensils that looked to have come from the hotel kitchen, plastic bags and tin cans and bottles . . .

Davis Deane had obviously used the swimming pool as his garbage dump, just as he'd cannibalized the hotel, selling off its furnishings and fixtures in order to eat. She wondered if it had hurt him to see the woodworking torn out, the chandeliers and mirrors taken down, everything carted away piecemeal. Or had he been beyond caring at that point, looking only for the price of another bottle of cheap liquor? Somehow she doubted that; after all, he'd described this place as the only thing he still cared about *besides* the bottle.

She shrugged her thoughts off and resumed her search.

All four guestrooms and connecting baths on the second floor were empty and stripped. On the third floor a few pictures hung lopsidedly on the walls. The air was drier up there, the smell of mold less pervasive. The windows were not boarded, and through one Joanna caught sight of the sun slanting across the neighboring vineyard, trailers of steam rising from the damp ground. She looked at her watch and was surprised to see it was nearly eight o'clock.

She went back downstairs, feeling even more discouraged than when she'd found nothing in the cabin. If Deane had stored his papers here in the hotel, he'd hidden them too cleverly for her to find. They must contain something extremely important, for him to have taken such precautions. Or perhaps he'd merely done so on an old man's somewhat paranoid whim.

She supposed she should leave, go to the hospital and see how Deane was after surgery, but instead she was drawn back to the courtyard. She hadn't examined it all that carefully; she'd check it one more time. But the only possible hiding place was an empty ivy-covered shed from which pool equipment had presumably been removed.

As she walked the length of the court, a depression that had little to do with not locating the papers descended on her. This courtyard was all that remained of the resort's days of glory, and its condition proved how long gone the Jazz Age was—as dead as most of the people who had lived through it. The trash in the pool, the ivy growing through cracks in the walls, the broken tiles and rotting latticework: They were testimony to the indifference with which time treats all things and people.

Funny, she thought, how up to this moment the wild days of Prohibition hadn't seemed so long ago. After all, when she'd first heard of them and become intrigued by the mix-

ture of fact and folklore, they'd been a mere thirty-some
years past. But then before she'd known it, three more decades had slipped by. Her own life, which had seemed to
stretch endlessly only years ago, was now half over. And
how had she spent it? In subterfuge, revenge, fear, resentment . . .

Suddenly she felt an intense weariness; she sat down on
the edge of the bandstand. Why didn't she just give up? she
thought. Quit fighting back, run away, start over somewhere else. She had money, more than enough to buy herself a new identity. She didn't need to worry about E.J. any
longer, had—as he claimed—been presumptuous to keep up
her protectiveness this long. He was embarking on his life's
work now and, angry as Parducci was at E.J.'s rejection of
him as his natural father, he would never harm his own son.
She herself was the one he wanted; if she vanished . . .

The sun had reached the greenhouse roof now. The
cracked panes shattered its rays into the reds and blues and
greens of the spectrum. Joanna glanced up, squinting
against the glare. A familiar sort of wire was strung just
under the roof's peak. The sort of wire that was part of a
burglar alarm system.

An alarm system, here in an abandoned hotel that hadn't
been operational since before such devices were commonly
used?

She got to her feet and followed the wire, craning her
neck. It extended the length of the peak in either direction,
branching off at intervals to the sides. At the bandstand end
of the courtyard it dropped down behind the latticework.

Quickly she went over there and examined the latticework more closely. Its center panel was really a door, with
only screwholes where a handle had once been. She pried at
its edges with her fingertips and pulled it open; the top hinge
was so loose that the door needed to be lifted and propped.

Inside was a small room, possibly for storing pool furniture or musicians' gear. It was now filled with cardboard file

boxes. The terminal for the burglar alarm—a simple type that hadn't been manufactured since the sixties—was attached to one wall.

Joanna lifted the lid on the box nearest her. It was crammed with manila files. She squatted down beside it and looked through them, reading their labels. Income tax records, bank statements, canceled checks—none of them dated later than 1968. A second box contained real estate escrow papers; a few others held business correspondence; the dates on them stopped in the early sixties. There were other cartons full of similar material: insurance policies, ledgers, annual reports, stock brokerage statements. At one time Deane had been a wealthy and organized man.

If she took the hours necessary to go through these, Joanna thought, she could probably piece together an interesting story concerning the financial downfall of Davis Deane. But she doubted they were the papers the old man had wanted her to look at.

Only a few boxes left. She crawled over to the next one and raised its lid. It contained newspaper clippings, letters, postcards, photographs, other mementos. A valentine with crumbling lace edges was signed "With Love from Bea." There were several faded blue and red ribbons from various wine competitions at the Sonoma County Fair. A diploma from Sonoma Valley High School certified that Peter Davis Deane had graduated with honors in 1937. An engraved wedding invitation announced the marriage of same Peter Davis Deane to Adele Ann Nelson in 1939. A photograph showed a middle-aged couple seated in an arbor that Joanna recognized as the one that still stood in the front yard of the East Napa Street house. The man was Deane; she supposed the pleasant, smiling woman was Bea of the sentimental valentine. The browned and brittle newspaper clippings confirmed that: Bea Deane had been an officer of the garden club and active on the committees of the First Methodist Church. Deane himself had led various civic

causes, and their son Peter—a serious, handsome young
man—had enlisted in the navy at the start of World War II.
Other clippings showed Deane with his fellow members of
the local civil defense unit and the sheriff's department
auxiliary. Still another, from the early sixties, announced his
appointment as acting chief of police; in reading the article, Joanna was surprised to find that the old man had had
a brief career in law enforcement in the 1920s, and thus had
been qualified to act as an interim replacement when the
Sonoma chief had died suddenly in 1960.

But interesting as all that was, these mementos were not
what she was looking for, either. She replaced them in the
box and turned to the next. When she opened it she saw it
was only half full; on top lay a clipping that looked fairly
recent. She unfolded it to a feature article from the San
Francisco *Examiner*, dated just one month ago.

RECORD ART AUCTION
SLATED FOR RENFROW'S

Joanna skimmed the piece, then read it more carefully. It
reported that Renfrow's Auctioneers, one of the two San
Francisco auction houses that approximated Christie's or
Sotheby's, had announced the pending sale of Vincent Van
Gogh's *Flowers along the Rhone* for Saturday, April 23. The
auction of one of the artist's most famous paintings was
expected to attract an international group of museum curators, dealers, and collectors; bids were expected to rival
those of previous record auctions of Van Gogh's work. The
proceedings would be covered by closed-circuit television in
order to accommodate the crowd, and telephone bids would
be accepted by representatives of the auction house's fine-
arts sales department. The sale would be a first for San
Francisco. Other record auctions had been held in New
York, London, and Los Angeles....

April 23 was tomorrow.

Joanna sat fingering the clipping. Her lack of knowledge of the upcoming sale both surprised and disconcerted her. In past years she would not only have known of it before it was announced in the papers, but would already have secured herself a seat. It would have been a topic of conversation for weeks in advance with friends such as Nick or Sally Jane, but in spite of the fact they must know about it, neither of them had mentioned it to her. Or perhaps she hadn't been listening; she certainly hadn't been reading the newspapers thoroughly. It all went to show how preoccupied and withdrawn she was, how tightly wrapped in her cocoon of fear.

This clipping was obviously what Davis Deane had intended for her to see, and if it had not been pointed out to her in connection with her inquiries after Parducci, she might not even have grasped its significance.

Although Van Gogh had been born in Holland near the Belgian frontier, one did not think of him as a Dutch painter, in the sense of Rembrandt or Hals. His greatest paintings had been done in France, and he was classified as a Post-Impressionist, a category closely associated with that country. But Van Gogh *had* been Dutch, and the acquisition of works of Dutch artists was what Parducci arranged for his select list of clients.

A tingle of excitement ran through Joanna. She looked down at the rest of the clippings in the box, then dropped the one she held inside and replaced the lid. She'd take the whole thing with her, look through them to see if there was anything more...

There was a thumping sound on the outer wall of the courtyard.

Joanna stood and peered through the latticework. She saw nothing. The sun's glare on the greenhouse roof was blinding now. She shaded her eyes, looked more closely...

And then the burglar alarm began clanging.

SEVEN

THE NOISE WAS deafening. Joanna clapped her hands over her ears, and stumbled out onto the bandstand.

She saw no one on the roof or in the courtyard. The alarm kept going, loud enough to be heard a long way off. She rushed back into the room, risked her right eardrum by uncovering it, and pushed the off switch on the terminal. Echoes rang, then faded to silence.

She peered through the latticework again. Nothing moved in the courtyard; the silence was total. Those old alarms, she knew, were unstable; a bird could have set it off, or an electrical short. But what about the thump she'd heard?

Well, if someone had been attempting to break into the court, the alarm would certainly have scared him off. But it would be best to leave quickly, before he came back, or someone else arrived to investigate. She picked up the file box and left the little room, closing the latticework as she'd found it.

The heels of her boots tapped loudly on the tiles; she went on tiptoe the rest of the way. Inside the hotel she set the file box down and locked the glass doors, pulling the heavy drapes over them. Then she moved quietly toward the entry.

She was about to step outside when she noticed a pickup truck pulled behind the trees at the edge of the graveled area. It was so far in their shadow that she couldn't make out its model or color—other than that it was light—or see if anyone was inside. The way it was parked made her doubt it belonged to someone who had merely been attracted by the alarm.

She drew back, looking down at the file box, then glancing around for a place to hide it. There was a doorway under the staircase—the kind that leads to a storage area. She hurried over, tugged it open, and shoved the box inside next to a stack of browned newspapers. When she looked out the door again, there was still no one visible. All she could hear was the sound of birds in the ravine and the distant hum of traffic on the highway.

After a moment she stepped out onto the portico and closed the door. The chain and padlock still rested under the old car. She was about to reach for them when she heard a noise to the side of the building. A rustling, as if someone were moving stealthily through the overgrown shrubbery.

Joanna dropped into a crouch and slipped behind the rear bumper of the car.

There were more rustling sounds and then a figure emerged from the foliage. It looked to be a man, dressed in a loose rain slicker and hat. He faced away from her, his head moving from side to side as if he were scanning the surrounding terrain. In his right hand he carried a newspaper-wrapped package.

Joanna leaned out, trying to get a better look at him. The man seemed about to turn when her foot slipped.

The sole of her boot scraped on the gravel. She pitched downward, whacking her chin on the car's bumper. As she pushed up, she heard the man rush in her direction. She whirled and fled across the parking lot into the grove.

The man's feet slapped on the gravel. She dodged through the trees. Her heels stuck in the thick mud; she pulled hard and one foot started to come out of its boot. She stumbled, grabbed at the boot, and jammed her foot back in.

Behind her she heard the man slide on the mud. She zigzagged around a clump of bushes and saw one of the cabins straight ahead. It had no doors or window glass, and the porch foundation had cracked into two tilted slabs. She sprinted for it, vaulted the gap in the concrete, and slipped inside.

The man had apparently fallen, but now his footfalls resumed. Joanna crouched beneath one of the windows, panting. The floor was warped and buckled; sections of board were missing. She crawled over to one of the holes, thinking to wriggle underneath. Not enough clearance.

She heard the man stop outside, breathing heavily. She held her own breath.

He remained where he was.

Joanna inched across the floor to the door to the back room.

The man's footsteps came toward the cabin.

She shot to her feet and ran to the back window. This one had glass in it—great jagged shards extending from the bottom of its rotten frame. She pulled her sweater sleeves down over her hands and punched at the glass. The pieces fell outward; she scrambled through the opening and jumped to the ground.

She landed on her feet, but her knees buckled. She went down on them; pain shot through the one she'd recently wrenched while riding her bicycle. She pushed up and ran into the thicket at the edge of the ravine.

Branches stung her face and thorns tore at her clothing. The ground sloped sharply; she ran headlong, gathering speed with each step. Her foot plunged into a hole and she pitched forward, landing on her side and rolling over and over into the ravine.

Something heavy and solid broke her fall. For a few seconds she lay stunned. Then, painfully, she struggled up onto her elbows and saw that the object was a tree stump. She was sprawled on a bed of smooth stones. Water trickled over them and soaked through her clothing.

She sucked in her breath, held it, listened for noises on the slope above.

Nothing. Only the rush of the stream.

Was he up there, listening too?

She waited, breathing shallowly. Still nothing. In a few minutes the birds resumed their harsh chorus.

Finally she moved to the muddy bank above the stones. She was soaked clear through now, cold and shivering. Her body ached and throbbed. Scrapes and cuts stung her skin. She rolled over onto her back, heedless of the mud, and stared up through the trees. A starburst of sun shone among their leaves.

Then, some distance off, an engine started up.

Joanna sat. The engine grew louder as it gained power, then fainter, and finally faded away.

Leaving—or merely a trick?

Five minutes went by. Ten. The birds' screeching and hollering remained uninterrupted. More time passed. There was no sound of a returning truck, no movement, however stealthy, in the underbrush.

After a few more minutes she got to her feet. One boot stuck in the mud. When she pulled it out, the heel came off.

"Screw it," she muttered. She sat down again, pulled both boots off, and left them on the ground. In her stocking feet she began walking along the weedy, slippery bank. She followed it upstream, to where the creek widened beside a clearing. In its center stood the ruins of the fabled dance pavilion.

No telling what color it once had been; now it was as gray and weathered as the hotel. Most of its gingerbreading had dropped away, leaving a gaunt skeleton. Ivy wound about its pillars and moss covered the concrete floor. Half the roof had caved in.

At any other time Joanna would have been delighted at the sight of such a relic. Now she merely stumbled toward it, sat down on its concrete steps. She wrapped her arms around her torso and shivered in spite of the sun that streamed into the clearing.

The man, she thought. Who was he? Not much to go on. Couldn't see his face. Build wasn't apparent in that loose slicker. What else? His voice?

All the time he'd chased her he'd never once called out. Why?

Was he afraid she'd recognize him by his voice?

But that didn't make sense. She'd only had moments to glimpse him; probably he'd been at the same disadvantage. No way to tell who she was from her car, either—she'd parked it well up the road.

Leave that for a moment, she told herself. The real question is—what was he doing here?

If he set off that alarm—and he probably did—he was trying to get into the hotel. Why? To vandalize it? Doubtful. Vandals run in packs, usually at night; mostly they're drunks or kids. Not this guy.

Why, then? Don't know.

The answer, she decided, might lie back at the hotel. She got up, took a final look at the dilapidated pavilion, and began to hunt for the stone stairway that supposedly scaled the side of the ravine. It was there under a tangle of vines, just as the spinners of local legend claimed.

She approached cautiously, moving from cabin to cabin, tree to tree, until she could see where the pickup had stood. It was gone, and no other vehicle was in sight. When she rounded the hotel, she saw that the chain and padlock had been replaced on the door. She dug in her pocket for the keys, then realized she'd left them in the padlock; when she tugged at the padlock, she found it secure. Anger rose, and she gave the door a good kick, badly stubbing her stockinged toes.

"Serves you right," she muttered as she hopped around in pain.

Then she realized she'd lost her shoulder bag someplace, too. Cursing, she retraced her flight path through the grove.

It was there, under a clump of manzanita. She picked it up and trudged back to where she'd left the Fiat.

Weariness had taken the edge off her earlier panic, and she drove down Highway 12 automatically. But when she stopped for the traffic light near the Sonoma Mission Inn, she began shaking. Her foot could barely press on the accelerator when the light turned green; then she applied too much pressure and screeched off, burning rubber.

She got the car under control, gripping the wheel firmly. Looked in the rearview mirror. And saw the red light of the county sheriff's car just behind her.

EIGHT

THE SHERIFF'S DEPUTY was very understanding when Joanna explained that her nerves were on edge because she'd had a flat tire and almost been hit by a truck while changing it. He said the truck driver ought to be shot for splattering a lady with mud; told her she should have called Triple A instead of changing a tire herself; cautioned her to drive more carefully in the future. Joanna thanked him for not ticketing her and drove the rest of the way home without incident.

E.J. hadn't returned. There was no note from him, and his bed in the little room off the kitchen, which he preferred to the more spacious ones upstairs, hadn't been slept in. She wasn't sure whether that was a bad sign or not. Her son had always been a wanderer; he might have spent the night in his sleeping bag at the winery. Or he might have stopped in at Mario's after he left the house and gone home with one of the women he knew from there. E.J.'s fondness for the ladies who frequented the bar had almost got him sacked on numerous occasions in the days when he worked there.

She went upstairs, threw her filthy clothes in the hamper, and took a long hot shower. When she stepped out, Herman was standing on his hind legs, one paw in the toilet; his favorite catnip mouse had sunk to the bottom of the bowl. She sighed and fished it out for him. He trotted off, purring. As she dried herself Joanna wondered if this behavior wasn't some feline variant on the raccoon's food-washing ritual. Or perhaps Herman was just insane. But it was possible that in some dim (and largely empty) recess of the catly brain, dropping one's toys in the toilet where they couldn't be reached made perfect sense. When you considered it, much of human endeavor wasn't any more explicable.

With that philosophical fix on the day, she dressed and went to the study to consult a few reference works and make a phone call. Then she scribbled a note for E.J.—"Gone to S.F."—and left it on the kitchen table. Let him think what he would; she couldn't wait around to explain herself. Then, heeding Herman's plaintive howls and Ermine's quietly reproachful looks, she fed the cats, took a handful of Triscuits for herself, and set off for Sonoma Valley Hospital.

The woman at the information desk said Deane had come through the operation in satisfactory condition and was now in recovery; he could have no visitors. Joanna said she was a relative. "No one—not even family," the woman replied. "If you like you can wait over there with your other relative."

Joanna looked where she pointed, at a slender woman with shoulder-length reddish gold hair who sat with her back to the desk. When she went over the woman glanced at her, and she recognized Karla Perelli, the pretty young wine broker with whom Joe Donatello had planned to meet on Wednesday afternoon. Joanna had met Karla briefly at a party at Sally Jane's during the Christmas holidays; since then they'd run into each other a few times at Flair for Hair, where they shared the same stylist. This morning Karla's normally pert face was solemn and pinched. She nodded at Joanna and looked away.

Joanna sat next to her. "You're here to see Davis Deane?" she asked.

The wine broker looked mildly surprised, but merely nodded again.

"The woman at the desk said you're a relative."

"He's my great-grandfather—when he chooses to acknowledge me." Karla shifted on her chair so she could see Joanna more easily, and recrossed her slim legs. She was dressed as attractively as ever, in a tan linen skirt and black blazer; her hair and makeup were quite perfect. Karla, Joanna sensed, was a woman who could easily achieve such an effect, no matter how early in the morning she was summoned by emergency.

Karla added, "Davis would probably be furious if he knew I was here, but I'm all the family he's got left, and I'm staying."

"Your grandfather was his son Peter?"

"Right. My grandfather died in World War Two; his plane was shot down in the Pacific a few months before my mother was even born. So that old buzzard in there—" she gestured behind her "—is the closest thing to a grandfather I've ever had. Not that he works at it."

"Why don't you get along with him?"

"I get along. He tries not to. Maybe I'm too much like my grandmother. He quit dealing with her back in the early sixties, and he wouldn't have anything to do with Mom, either."

"Why not?"

If Karla found Joanna's questions intrusive or odd, she didn't show it. Probably she was glad to have someone to talk to while waiting. "Grandma remarried after the war— to Robert Donatello."

"Joe's grandfather?"

"You know Joe? Of course you do. E.J. Stark's your son. Yes, the same Robert Donatello. And there's another old buzzard for you: He rules that family with an iron claw. Joe and Veronica's parents—the old man's only son and his wife—were killed in a private plane crash when Joe was only five. The kids were with them; they survived. It's my theory that their grandfather has tried to turn both of them into replacements for his precious son. With Veronica, he may have succeeded. Joe's another story."

"But why did Davis cut your grandmother and mother off? Didn't he approve of Robert Donatello?"

"Initially he must have; they were close friends. Then they had a falling-out. They've been feuding for close to twenty-five years. After all this time no one really knows what caused it; I suspect neither of them even remembers. But there's so much bad blood that Davis didn't attend Grandma's funeral. He wouldn't have been welcome, I guess. When Mom died last year, he sent flowers, but he didn't show up for the service."

"So why are you here?"

Karla shrugged. "As I said, I'm all the family he's got. Plus I kind of like the old man. After my mother died I started this campaign to make him deal with me. I'd show up at the decrepit resort once a month and bring him a bottle of wine."

"What was his reaction?"

"The first time he ordered me off his land with a shotgun. The second time he kept the wine but ran me off just the same. Finally he let me sit on the porch with him while he drank it, then told me to bring bourbon if I came again. Nowadays he gives me a drink, too. But he won't admit that I'm any relation of his; he pretends I'm some crazy woman whom he tolerates because she won't let him alone."

Joanna smiled. "Cantankerous, isn't he?"

"I take it you know him."

"I only met him last night, but I feel as if we've been friends for a long time."

"He's that way, if you're his kind of person. He likes to think he's gruff and tough, but if you don't let yourself be intimidated by his facade, you'll find that a pussycat lurks within."

Joanna nodded. "Do you know how his accident happened?"

"Just that he ran off the road in the rain." Karla looked at her watch, glanced over at the desk. "I wish they'd tell me how he's doing. I need to know he's going to be all right."

When she looked at Joanna again, her hazel eyes were shiny with tears. "You see," she said, "he's all I've got left, too."

BEFORE SHE LEFT town, Joanna tracked Sally Jane down at the Good Earth Restaurant across from the newspaper offices. Her friend was drinking coffee and eating an enormous hero sandwich. Joanna got coffee and sat down across from her. The reporter looked cheerful and alert, even though she'd been on the job since before five.

"You go up to Deane's?" she asked.

"Yes."

"Find what he wanted you to?"

"Sort of. Sally Jane, did you say anything to me about the Van Gogh auction that Renfrow's is holding tomorrow?"

"I mentioned it a couple of times. You didn't seem interested."

"That worries me—I don't remember you talking about it."

"No big deal. You were preoccupied, is all. Nothing there for the likes of you and me, anyway. Even with your bucks, you can't ante up fifty or sixty million."

"Is that what they expect it'll bring?"

"If the bidding holds true to form."

"That's obscene!"

Sally Jane nodded, looking more concerned with the way her sandwich was falling apart than the implications of inflationary art prices.

Joanna said, "I was over at the hospital checking on Deane. He made it through surgery and is in recovery. Karla Perelli was there. I didn't realize she was related to him— and to the Donatellos."

"Well, only by her grandmother's marriage to old Robert. He never adopted her mother. There's bad blood there, too: The only one of the clan who will deal with her or Deane is Joe."

"Why?"

"Who knows? Feuding seems to be in the genes with these winemaking families—or maybe it's got something to do with hanging around the vats too much while the grapes're fermenting."

"Did you talk to the sheriff's department about Deane's accident?"

"Uh-huh. Probably happened around midnight, judging from his degree of exposure. Was driving south on Highway Twelve, between Glen Ellen and the resort. Went into the ditch around Trinity Road."

"He hadn't been drinking in Boyes?"

"Drinking, yes. But in Boyes, no. And here's something interesting: He was fairly lucid when they brought him in—well, you know that because he talked to me. He told the ambulance attendant that he was forced off the road by another truck."

Joanna waited. When Sally Jane didn't go on, she said, "And?"

"That's it. The attendant reported it to the S.O. My contact there tends to discount it. There was no evidence at the scene, and Deane was kind of raving, anyway."

Joanna thought of the pickup truck pulled back under the trees at Madrone Springs Resort. And of the man who had pursued her into the ravine. She bit her lip and glanced at her watch. "Listen, I have an appointment in the city. Will you do me a favor?"

"Sure."

"Keep in contact with the sheriff's department and the hospital. I'll call you later to see if there's anything more on this."

"Will do. When are you going to tell me what's going on?"

"Soon. I promise."

As Joanna went out the door, Sally Jane was eyeing a tray of pastries on the counter.

NINE

SONOMA IS FORTY-FIVE MILES from downtown San Francisco. A fast driver can make the trip in under an hour if the roads aren't jammed with slow vehicles full of rubbernecking tourists...if traffic doesn't come to a standstill at the perpetual highway construction zone around San Rafael...if there are no wrecks on the Golden Gate Bridge...if all the toll booths are open....

Today everything worked in Joanna's favor; by quarter to one she was searching for a parking space on Sutter Street in the city's gallery district. While the faint of heart would simply have pulled into the large parking structure at the corner of Stockton and walked uphill, Joanna prowled the curbs, heedless of the irate honks of motorists behind her, enjoying the hunt.

There was a woman struggling with too many packages; surely she was going to...another shop. That man was running—because his meter had expired? No, for a bus. A-hah—an empty space! No, a yellow zone. But that woman—the one with the briefcase—was checking her watch; in her hand she held keys. Bingo!

Joanna stopped while the woman got into her car, fussed with the seatbelt, started up. A man in a BMW behind her leaned on his horn. His face, glimpsed in her rearview mirror, was twisted into an ugly grimace as he mouthed obscenities at her. Joanna waited.

The other car exited the space. Joanna drove in. The BMW pulled alongside her, and the man gave her the finger. She returned it cheerfully, waved as he screeched off.

City life...and people wondered why she had moved to Sonoma!

She locked the car, fed the meter, and walked two blocks to a short sidestreet north of Sutter. Although she'd been there often she never could remember its name. Today she meant to check and fix it firmly in her mind, but when she got there she found the building on the corner was being painted; the street sign that normally hung on its wall had been removed. Perhaps, she thought, it was a warning from the powers that be (whoever they were) not to tax her brain with unnecessary details.

Around the corner was La Cocina Restaurant. She'd always thought it a dumb name—The Kitchen Restaurant—but they served the best *chiles rellèños* in town. Just sniffing the air in the foyer made her mouth water.

Adam Hawthorne, president and major stockholder of Renfrow's Auctioneers, waited for her in his usual booth, looking too aristocratic for words. His blue suit was sartorially correct; his striped tie hinted at an Ivy League education; his wavy gray hair, clear blue eyes, and evenly tanned skin all proclaimed him the product of generations of WASPish inbreeding. When the maître d' led her to the table, Adam stood, motioning for her to be seated with a graciousness that nannies attempt to instill in their small charges before they are able to walk.

"Hi, toots," he said in his thick Brooklyn accent. "Whaddaya want from the bar?"

Joanna accepted his welcoming kiss on her cheek, sat down, and said, "White wine, please."

Adam gestured at a hovering waiter. "Bring her half a carafe—the woman's a lush."

The waiter—young and obviously new there, since he looked scandalized by Adam's behavior—scurried away.

Adam leaned back and took a sip of his margarita. He studied Joanna over the glass's salt-caked rim and nodded—whether in satisfaction with the drink or her appearance, she couldn't tell. "About time you gave me a call," he said. "Where've you been keeping yourself this past year?"

"Sonoma. I've been . . . busy and haven't managed to get down here much."

"Not renovating another house?"

"God, no!"

"So what brings you to town? It couldn't have anything to do with my auction, could it?"

"Um, yes."

"Craven woman. I suppose you want a front row seat." Renfrow's reserved several rows for favored customers.

"Any seat will do."

"Don't go humble on me. You've got it." The waiter arrived. He fussed over pouring the wine to the correct level and arranging the carafe just so. Adam said, "That's okay, Eric. She's going to drink it, not paint a picture of it."

Eric flushed, set down a pair of menus, and fled.

"Nice kid," Adam said, "but he makes me nervous as hell. I keep thinking he'll settle down and start enjoying the work, but he's been here three months, and still he's as jumpy as a minister in a hot-sheet motel."

"The nervousness is mutual, then."

"Yeah. But why? I'm not an ogre. Am I?"

"You can be . . . abrupt. And outspoken."

Adam shrugged. "Nothing I can do about that. I just turned fifty yesterday; I'm too damn old to change."

"No one wants you to. And happy birthday."

"Thanks. Got a birthday kiss for an old man?"

Joanna leaned over and attempted to kiss him on the cheek. Adam turned his head and their lips met. Now he was making *her* nervous. She'd known him for a number of years, ever since David had been adding to his Impressionist collection and had bought a number of items through Renfrow's. From the beginning she'd sensed that Adam nursed a carefully restrained but steadily burning lust for her. And she'd always suspected that his interest made her uneasy because it wasn't wholly unreciprocated.

To cover her discomfort she sipped wine and reached for the menu.

With a hint of amusement Adam said, " What—you're not gonna have the rellños?"

"The...yes, of course." She set the menu down unopened. "I swear I'm getting more and more forgetful lately. Little things, like the name of this street and the fact that I always have the rellños here. Things like walking into a room and not remembering what I went in there for."

"Happens to all of us." Adam's lean tanned face took on a slightly melancholy cast, and he covered her hand with his. "We're not getting any younger, toots. Neither of us has got time to waste."

The words were incongruous with his appearance. If anything, Adam looked better than the last time she'd seen him. His touch unsettled her, and she tried to pull her hand away.

A year ago she'd sworn off men—maybe not for good, but certainly until she felt strong enough to cope with the upheaval and excitement and—regrettably—the eventual disillusionment that an affair usually brought. She wasn't at all sure she'd recovered that strength yet, and what little she possessed would be needed to deal with Parducci.

"Relax," Adam said. "Even your late husband considered me a gentleman."

She glanced at him, saw the wry self-mocking smile she remembered from many previous meetings. It put her in mind of Davis Deane, when he'd spoken of his evenings at Rosa's Tavern, and she was pleasantly surprised to realize that in Adam she'd found another kindred spirit. She squeezed his hand, took hers away, and said, "I hope all this talk about aging isn't evidence that you're having your mid-life crisis."

"That? I had it in my thirties when I sold my antiques business, left my wife, moved away from Brooklyn, and changed my name."

More than fifteen years earlier when Adam had entered the high-stakes art game, he'd decided it wasn't yet ready for a man named Harvey Kowerduck. So (with characteristic lack of modesty) he'd changed his first name to Adam, after the first man, and his surname to Hawthorne, after the author of *The Scarlet Letter* (the novel about adultery being the only work of literature that he'd ever read all the way through). Over the years he'd acquired a considerable knowledge of art, high finance, high society, and fine food and wine; he was respected by dealers, collectors, and artists alike; he owned a home in San Francisco and a horse ranch in West Marin; he contributed generously to museums, supported several needy artists, and had established an art scholarship at a local college. Seemingly, he had achieved it all.

Except, as he was quick to point out, he had never found the right woman. And he'd never got rid of that Brooklyn accent.

Reflecting on his escape from his former life seemed to cheer him. He signaled to Eric the waiter and ordered for both of them. Then he poured more margarita from the pitcher in front of him and said, "Tell you what—after the auction I'll take you to dinner. We'll celebrate Renfrow's breaking into the big time."

"You think this sale will do that?"

"It'll make us another Butterfield and Butterfield." He named San Francisco's most prominent auction house.

"How's your security setup?"

"Tight, damned tight."

"I hope a good firm's handling it."

He raised an eyebrow. "You're not angling for us to steer our future business SSI's way?"

"I wouldn't mind of you did. But, no, this isn't a pitch. I'm not really all that involved in the company any more."

Now Adam frowned. "What, you've heard talk on the street that something might go down?" Like many of her old friends, Adam knew that Joanna maintained a fair number of contacts in the art underworld; she supposed that from time to time he wondered why, but he'd never asked.

"No." She shook her head, toyed with the stem of her wineglass. Finally she said, "I *have* heard that there's a European broker in the area, one who's more or less specialized in Dutch art. And while Van Gogh isn't what he's typically gone after—"

"Which broker is that?"

"Antony Parducci."

"Uh-huh. I remember something about him—and you. When they had that mess at the de Young a couple of years ago, and the scandal involving—"

"That's right." It was a time Joanna didn't want to think about, much less discuss.

Adam must have caught the finality in her voice. He merely said, "I'll alert my head of security. And thanks for telling me."

She nodded. Their lunches arrived—relleños for her, *carne asada* for him—and for a few minutes they fell silent.

"So," she said, after sampling the chiles and finding them as she remembered, "tell me about the Van Gogh. The newspaper said it was one of his most famous paintings, but it's not one I know. I looked it up in my reference works and found very little on it."

"The newspaper embellished, I'm afraid. It's an excellent painting, but it sure as hell isn't famous, or even one of his best. It was done in 1889, after he went to the asylum at Saint-Remy." Van Gogh had gone voluntarily to the institution, where he'd experienced a year of great productivity; he'd died a suicide after leaving there in 1890.

"What's its provenance?" Joanna asked.

"It's been in a private collection for about twenty-five years. Before that it's kind of hazy."

"Does that bother you?"

"Not particularly. Even if there once was a cloud over its ownership, after twenty-five years it's legally clean." The statute of limitations for stolen artworks varied from country to country, ranging from three to ten years; one of the aims of groups trying to curtail theft was the establishment of a uniform worldwide legal limit.

"So," Joanna said, "its provenance could conceivably have been bleached by this collector sitting on it."

Annoyance flickered in Adam's eyes. "Could have, but we're confident the owner has full legal right to it. If not, given the publicity the sale's had, someone would have stepped forward by now. I'm afraid you've been fooling around with crooks too long, toots." Although his words were light, there was an edge to them.

Joanna could understand his irritation at her statement. The gray area in the world of art dealing was very large indeed; even establishments such as Renfrow's frequently strayed into it. She'd noticed of late that a number of tactful expressions of uncertainty as to the authenticity of various works had been inserted into the text of their catalogs: A lithograph had been attributed to "Dali," rather than "Salvador Dali;" a stained glass panel had been attributed to "L. C. Tiffany," rather than "Louis Comfort Tiffany." These were subtle insider's hints aimed at the discerning collector, indicating that while the artwork's owner had believed in its authenticity, the auction house's staff of experts had their reservations. The practice was time-honored and widespread. Salvador Dali himself had once complained that a well-known auction house often neglected to send him their catalogs when they were having a sale of his works, for fear some of them might turn out to be fakes.

Joanna hastened to smooth over her tactless remark. "I didn't mean to imply that you would knowingly auction a painting with a clouded provenance."

"I know. We're just touchy about things like that lately. There was that recent rash of photomechanical lithographs being passed off as the real thing. And the collection of Himalayan artifacts belonging to the murdered drug dealer that Butterfield's had on the block last month. The guy had rightful title to them, but there was plenty of talk about how he got the money to buy them—and where the proceeds were going."

Joanna remembered the incident: Numerous law enforcement agencies, both federal and local, had been standing in line for a cut of the sale profits. "Well, you aren't dealing with anyone like that, I trust. Who *is* the owner?"

Adam sipped his margarita, set it down, and smiled.

"He doesn't want his identity known?" she asked.

"Nope."

"Oh, come on—tell me. You know it won't go any farther."

"I might, but it depends."

"On what?"

"On whether you'll agree to have dinner with me after the sale."

"I will, I promise." She had been planning to accept his invitation anyway.

"The seller is Jerome Eckridge."

In one way it didn't surprise her; in another it did. Jerry Eckridge was someone she knew casually—one of the city's more affluent collectors, who had attended the same gallery and museum openings she and David went to. It had been . . . five years? six? . . . since she'd last seen him.

Eckridge was a man from a poor background who had married the only daughter of the founder of a large Oakland-based shipping line. He'd taken the job his father-in-law had tossed him as a sop for signing a prenuptial agreement and built a power base from which he eventually took over the company. Eckridge Shipping, as it was now called, was a leader in the containerized freight field, and Jerry Eckridge was a very wealthy man. Joanna couldn't imagine why he would be disposing of such a valuable painting as the Van Gogh; it must be the pride of his collection.

"What's going on with Jerry?" she asked. "Is he in financial trouble?"

"Poor bastard's fighting both a divorce and a hostile takeover of the shipping line."

"Sandra finally left him?" Jerry Eckridge was a notorious womanizer—but then his wife hadn't been any too faithful, either. Joanna remembered a dinner party at which David had been seated next to Sandra; afterward he'd confided that she kept putting her hand on his thigh throughout the meal. David, who had a strong conservative bent when it came to such matters, admitted that he'd been too horrified to do anything but pretend it wasn't happening.

Adam said, "She left two months ago, and is taking him to the cleaners. Some people say she and her latest lover are the ones behind the takeover attempt. Anyway, Jerry's liquidating whatever assets are his separate property."

"Did he ask you to set up an off-the-wall bid?" Occasionally an auction house arranged for a dummy bid to be submitted—either by mail, telephone, or a ringer in the hall. It served the dual purpose of driving the bidding up and making the painting officially worth a certain amount, a fact that could be added to its provenance. Should the bid not be topped, the auction house would merely hold the painting for a while, then resell it with the dummy bid as the floor price.

"No," Adam said, "we're starting with a straight minimum bid of seventeen million. I'm confident the hammer price will be much higher."

"How much?"

"Hard to say. But given today's market I'd estimate upward of sixty-five million."

"Jesus. Plus ten percent for your commission, and the buyer will be looking at a total outlay of seventy-one point five million!"

Adam smiled wolfishly. "Yeah. Six point five million in commission should put us squarely in the big time, don't you think?"

She nodded.

"Yeah," he repeated, "that'd buy a lot of lentils."

"A lot of *what*?"

"Lentils." He spread his hands self-deprecatingly. "What can I say? You can take the boy out of Brooklyn—"

"What night of the week did you have lentil soup?"

"Thursday. Night before payday."

"We had it on Saturday, because my mother always saved up for a roast on Sunday. The way I knew my father's law practice had gotten successful was when lentil soup disappeared from the menu."

"Well, I'll be damned."

Joanna studied him, looking beyond his urbane, made-over facade to Harvey Kowerduck. He would have been what they now called a nerd: skinny, with impossibly curly hair; possessed of a sallow complexion from spending too much time inside; dressed in hand-me-downs or thrift-shop specials. He would have preferred reading to team sports, solitude to congregating on the front steps with the other kids, and would have saved his allowance for trips to the museum rather than the movies. Above all, he would have nursed a burning passion to get away from lentil soup, cream soda, fifth-floor walk-ups, and kids who taunted him with the nickname "coward duck."

"I'll be damned," he said again and reached for her hand.

She smiled and entwined her small fingers in his long slender ones.

TEN

AFTER SHE LEFT ADAM, Joanna fed her parking meter again and walked downhill to the Halsey gallery on lower Grant Avenue near Union Square. She gave her card to one of the salesmen and waited next to a display of nineteenth-century Japanese lacquer inros—boxes, for carrying personal items, that hang on the sash of the kimono. The information card for the central item in the case claimed it had been the property of one of the emperor's courtesans; the languid gold figure of a seated woman glittered against the box's glowing black finish. While it—like all the objects on display—was unquestionably tasteful and elegant, it failed to stir Joanna's interest. She preferred strength in artworks, some motion, even conflict. Japanese art was too delicate and static for her taste.

But there, she thought, she was definitely in the minority; Oriental art was enjoying an upswing, as evidenced by the number of customers who appeared to be doing more than browsing. Joanna studied them, wondering how many knew that gallery owner Malcolm Halsey was, as they said in the trade, more than a little "bent."

The salesman returned and ushered her to a back room—more a study than an office—where Halsey held court amidst his collection of some five hundred umbrellas. The diminutive dealer—he stood at less than five feet—had a passion for umbrellas and never appeared without one, rain or shine. His collection ranged from the simple to the ornate; their handles and tips were of carved wood, ivory, silver, and gold; several were encrusted with precious stones; their only commonality was that they were all black.

No one knew why Halsey had such a fascination with black umbrellas, but of course rumors abounded: They were symbolic of looking at life pessimistically, always expecting rain; they were a clever visual pun on the term *tax shelter*; they were a sexual fetish . . .

It was Joanna's theory that Halsey merely collected umbrellas the way others collect teacups, stamps, or books. As for their being black, up until recent decades most umbrellas had come in only that hue, and those that were manufactured in brighter colors were usually tacky. As for Halsey constantly carrying an umbrella, it was probably a shrewd promotional device calculated to keep the rumors flowing and his gallery in the public eye. If he was anything, Malcolm Halsey was shrewd.

As she entered the room, the dealer came around his mahogany desk and extended his delicate hand to her, then seated her in one of a pair of brocade chairs in front of the tiled Victorian fireplace. The umbrellas—in specially constructed display racks—covered all four walls; the collection had grown since the last time she'd visited. Halsey offered wine and busied himself at a cart, extracting a cork from an iced bottle of Chardonnay. In his correct black suit, with his thinning black hair and pencil-fine mustache, he looked like a little waiter doll whose enameled features had been painted on with a brush. Joanna started to smile and looked away so he wouldn't see her amusement.

After he brought the drinks, Halsey sat in the other chair, sipped wine, and pronounced it good. "The winery is a new one in Anderson Valley," he added. "One in which I hold a small interest. I hear you've recently become a vintner yourself."

As ever, Joanna was surprised at the wealth of gossip Halsey managed to tap into. "Hardly," she said. "I'm just helping my son get started."

Halsey raised his eyebrows. "I thought the boy was your stepson."

She hesitated. In her former San Francisco circle, it wasn't generally known that David had adopted E.J.—much less that she was his natural mother. In Sonoma she'd become used to referring to him as her son, but doing so in San Francisco would generate talk and necessitate explanations that she didn't care to offer. She merely replied, "After all these years, the distinction has blurred."

Halsey nodded. "If you raise a child, he becomes your own. Now—to what do I owe the honor? Since you sent in your business card, am I right in assuming you're here on behalf of SSI?"

"Yes." Joanna sipped wine before beginning her slightly fictionalized explanation. "I'm doing a favor for Adam Hawthorne. Something to do with tomorrow's sale."

"You say a favor. SSI isn't handling the security for Renfrow's, then?"

"No, but Adam is an old friend. I've come to you to ask if you've heard any rumors that something might go down."

Halsey's gallery was legitimate, but he was always willing to steer a customer to associates whose dealings were tainted—providing he received a share of the commission when the client acquired the special object he or she sought. His contacts on the street and throughout the art underworld were wide and—because of a seemingly limitless and unspecified debt to her late husband—he had always been willing to share what he heard with Joanna, providing it jeopardized no plans of his own.

Now he pursed his lips and closed his eyes in concentration. After a moment he said, "I've heard nothing."

"This is a very important sale. Whatever arrangements are being made will have been kept extremely quiet."

"But there would have been some hint. There always is."

"All the same, could you ask around?"

"Of course. You'll need the information as soon as possible, I assume?"

"Yes."

Halsey nodded absently and closed his eyes again.

Joanna sipped wine, waiting.

After a moment he said, "There is one contact I can ask who is sure to have heard if anything is being arranged—and who is discreet enough that I won't find myself responsible for starting a rumor. Call me here at five, and I'll have an answer for you." He raised his glass, regarding her curiously over its rim.

"I have never understood why I keep supplying information to you, Mrs. Stark," he said. "It's true that I once owed your late husband a great deal, but I'm sure he would consider the debt repaid by now."

"Why do you, then?"

He shrugged. "As I said, I don't know. In a way, the impulse is similar to the reason I collect black umbrellas. Despite all the exotic rumors that are bruited about, I haven't the foggiest idea why I acquire the damned things. It's just something I *do*, that's all."

BY THE TIME she arrived at Islais Creek Resort, the lunchtime rush was long over. The dilapidated frame building that leaned drunkenly beside a stagnant channel in the eastern industrial sector of the city was currently enjoying a vogue as an eatery, much as its sister restaurants, Mission Rock Resort and The Ramp, had in years past. As Joanna entered, a tipsy couple in business attire were descending the stairway from the second-story deck. The woman clung to the man's arm and giggled; he was fishing a package of breath mints from his pocket. Joanna gave them a wide berth as she crossed to the downstairs bar and poolroom.

The lower story reflected the true character of the place, and it was there that the owner, Tony Capello, spent most of his time after the upper bar and dining area cleared out. The downstairs was populated all day long by a motley crew of surly men who seemed to exist on unemployment checks and what they won at pool. Beer and hard liquor were the

only libations available; anyone requesting food, wine or
nonalcoholic drinks were none too politely shown the door.
Over the years the bar had been tended by a series of ex-
convicts who were even less communicative than their customers; a fringe group of indigent artists from studios in the
nearby converted warehouses often congregated on the ad-
joining deck. The low level of the resort's downstairs clientele was not accidental: Capello cultivated them, extending
credit and doling out occasional free meals. For this lar-
gesse, he expected to be repaid—by their willingness to per-
form various illicit jobs, which frequently included art
thefts.

When Joanna entered, Capello was racking the balls on
one of the two pool tables. The bartender—a new one since
the last time she'd visited—didn't even glance at her; the
three customers on the stools remained inert. It was not, she
thought, that the men who frequented the downstairs were
actively sexist; they simply didn't see women, didn't see
much of anything beyond the next drink and game of pool.

Tony Capello looked up, however. Did a double take.
And said, "Oh shit, not you again!"

"Me again," she said cheerfully.

Capello shook his bald head and drew his shaggy eyebrows together. In the year and a half since she'd last seen
him, his brows seemed to have become bushier, while his
grizzled fringe of hair had shrunk. He planted his short legs
wide apart, folded his arms over the mound of his beer belly,
and said, "I thought I finally got rid of you. Go away."

"Tony, is that any way to talk to an old friend?"

"Friend—bullshit! I told you the last time, I don't owe
you any more. So now you come around wanting something."

"Who says I do?" She reached for a cue and the chalk.

"*I* say it. You didn't come here for no game of pool."

"Five bucks a game, eight-ball. You break." Pool had
been the one form of amusement in her father's otherwise

staid and humorless existence, and she'd learned to play when she was barely tall enough to reach the table. Later her enthusiasm for the game had prompted David to buy a billiards table. While it had remained in the San Francisco house when she'd sold it, recently she'd taken to playing now and then at a bar on the plaza with Mary Bennett.

Capello glared at her, then shrugged and reached for his cue. Probably he thought she would be an easy opponent. He set the cue ball to the left of center and broke cleanly, dropping the nine into the far right pocket.

"So how've you been, Tony?"

"Great—until you walked in." He lined up his shot and sank the twelve ball.

"I see you've got a new bartender."

"He's been here a while, since Dan got sent back to Q."

She didn't know which of the seedy procession of employees the hapless Dan had been, but she said, "Oh yeah? How come?"

"None of your damn business." Capello leaned over the cue ball. "Ten ball." It dropped easily—a straight-in shot. He studied the table, moved around to the far side.

Joanna leaned against the wall next to the cue rack. "You still doing favors for friends?" she asked. It was the way Capello liked to describe his sideline; in law enforcement parlance, he was very close to a "fagin"—one who managed a string of thieves and arranged for them to pull jobs in exchange for a cut of their fees.

Capello frowned and moved to his right before leaning over the table. "That's none of your business, either."

Joanna said, "I hear there's something big going down before the Renfrow's auction tomorrow."

Capello's cue shot forward; the fourteen ball rolled toward the pocket but hung on the lip. "Damn you! You said that just to throw me off."

"No, I didn't. It's what I've heard."

"You're a liar."

"No, I'm not. You must be slipping, Capello, if you don't know about it."

She moved toward the table. Capello glared at her, but she saw a flicker of uncertainty in his eyes. She tapped the cue ball into the six and sank it easily.

"If you're not slipping," she said, "how come you don't know as much as I do?"

"Because there *ain't* nothing to know, that's why."

"As you say, bullshit."

"Don't you bullshit me, you pipsqueak broad. Just because somebody taught you to install a burglar alarm, it don't mean you know anything."

Joanna said, "Three ball—cross bank."

Capello grimaced as the three rolled into the side pocket.

"I guess you're just all washed up, Capello," she added.

"Someday you're gonna go too far, the way you talk."

"Probably." She spotted a relatively easy three-ball combination. Although she wasn't at all sure she could make it, just trying would raise her a notch in Capello's estimation. She took her time studying it, then said, "Two ball. Combination off the four off the seven."

Capello's eyes widened. She grinned up at him, then leaned over, studied some more, and stroked. The balls connected just right and dropped one after the other into three different pockets.

Capello said, "What the fuck—you buy yourself a table so you can practice every day?"

Joanna masked her own pleased surprise. "Just takes natural talent." After that, the next three balls would be easy.

"So what do you think, Capello?" she asked, lining up the five ball. "*Is* something going to go down before this time tomorrow?"

"No." But there was an undertone of worry in his voice. Capello had always prided himself on knowing everything that was going on.

She sank the five and moved around the table.

"I'd have heard," Capello said. "I hear everything."

"One ball. You *used* to hear everything."

"Will you stop it with the 'used to' crap?"

The one dropped. "Eight ball, side pocket."

Capello had lost interest in the game. He went to the door to the deck and stared out toward the shipyards across the channel.

Joanna stroked, put the eight and the game away. "You owe me five bucks, Tony."

He turned, sighing in exasperation. "You had to come here, ruin my day."

"You can't expect to win all the time."

"I'm not talking about pool, and you know it." He took a wad of bills from his pocket, peeled off a five, and threw it on the table.

Joanna said, "Rack them again?"

"Shit, no."

"Come on—I'll double the bet."

"I said no. Just what is it you really want, anyway?"

"I came here with the idea of finding out more about what's going down at Renfrow's. But like you said before, you don't owe me any more. And you don't know anything, anyway."

Capello's gaze shifted to a point beyond her left shoulder. Joanna glanced that way, too. The bartender and his three customers were watching intently—probably had been watching all along. Capello's jaw firmed. "I'll check it out," he said. "If I'm right—if nothing's going down—you owe me ten times that." He motioned at the bill on the table.

Joanna picked it up, folded it, and stuck it in her jacket pocket. "You've got a bet."

Really, she thought, it was a good bit less than she'd been prepared to pay him outright for the same information.

SSI's OFFICES were in a reasonably antiquated narrow stone building on Market Street near Fifth. Bill, the security man in the lobby, was almost as old as the structure itself. This afternoon Joanna discovered he was getting deaf. When she said, "Hi, Bill, how've you been?" he replied, "You bet it's a sin, the way those politicians are ruining this country." For a moment she was nonplussed, until she saw that he had his small portable TV tuned to a news commentary.

"Yes, it is." She signed his clipboard and headed for the elevator. "And something ought to be done about it."

Bill said, "Fun? Ain't nothing fun about it!"

When she entered SSI's seventh-floor offices, Phyllis Pryor, their secretary, greeted her with genuine pleasure. Phyllis was a thin birdlike woman of indeterminate age, efficient and gracious, but possessed of a reserve that at times could be off-putting. Today she unbent and said, "We've missed you. I know Nick's been hoping you'd make it down here this week. Shall I buzz him?"

"No, I want to make some phone calls first. Then I'll surprise him."

She went down the corridor to her office, past the conference room where their fluctuating staff of field consultants worked. As always she felt she was returning to a home where a welcome had been prepared for her. Her desk was polished and orderly; her photographs of David, E.J., and herself hung straight on the walls; the glass cases filled with souvenirs of various travels looked to have recently been dusted. The office seemed to cry out for her to resume permanent residence, yet for close to five years now, she had sat at the desk only intermittently.

Now she moved briskly around it, thumbed through her Rolodex, and dialed a number. Jerry Eckridge's private secretary informed her that he was out of town and would be unavailable until Monday. She left her name in case he called in within the next hour, but doubted she'd hear from him. Next she tried E.J. and Sally Jane, but was unable to reach either. Karla Perelli was in her office in the yellow Victorian on Sonoma's main street where she both lived and worked; she reported her great-grandfather to be in critical but stable condition. Karla sounded listless and depressed; she had another call and cut the conversation off abruptly.

After she hung up, Joanna considered trying Sally Jane again, but she had left SSI's number both at the newspaper and on the reporter's machine. E.J. was another matter. She called the house again, let the phone ring fifteen times. The winery phone had been due to be installed today, and E.J. had given her the preassigned number, but it also rang without answer.

It was nearing five o'clock—time to go down the hall to Nick's office before he fled to the hilltop retreat he shared with his woman friend in Sausalito. When she entered, he sat slumped in his chair, feet propped on a pulled-out file cabinet drawer, staring out the window. It opened onto the alley and provided an excellent view of the offices in the adjacent building; the only visible occupant was an attractive redheaded woman who was walking about, talking on a cordless phone and gesturing emphatically. After she made a particularly sweeping motion with her right hand, Nick said, "You tell him, baby!"

Joanna said, "Men used to spy on women wearing sexy underwear. Now you're all into watching power plays."

Nick started and his foot slipped off the drawer. He swiveled toward her, a grin spreading across his craggy face. "Power's always been sexy," he said. "We just didn't use to realize how it enhances the beauty of members of the opposite gender—to say nothing of their earning abilities."

"As you should well know." Nick's live-in was CEO of a major food importer; her income was many times in excess of his.

"I never claimed I couldn't be bought. But this is great— you've finally returned to the fold. Did you have time to go over the printout I brought you?"

Joanna had totally forgotten it. She supposed it was still on the desk in her study, where E.J. had put it when he found the telltale file box. "Uh, no. I plan to get to it the first of next week. What I'm down here for is the auction at Renfrow's." As she spoke she realized she needed to call Malcolm Halsey within the next fifteen minutes.

"I couldn't even get a pass," Nick said. "How'd you manage it?"

"Adam Hawthorne."

He raised his eyebrows. "Hawthorne, eh? I've always suspected he had a thing for you."

"Don't get all excited—it's only a pass to the auction. But I did drop a hint that SSI might be willing to take on Renfrow's security."

"Bless you. That new man we've got—Peale—would make a perfect fit." Nick, she could tell, was already planning how SSI would handle the account. "Jo, their business would put this firm solidly in the black. Couldn't you just . . . you know? I mean it—the guy's got the hots—"

"Only if the spirit moves me. Right now I want to discuss how much in the black we are. That way, when I go over the printout, it'll make more sense."

They spent the next ten minutes discussing SSI's financial health; like Davis Deane's condition, it could be described as critical but stable. Nick was a poor manager at best, and of late had been too enamored of his luxurious Sausalito life-style to keep a firm hand on the reins of the business. As Nick left for the day and she went back to her own office, Joanna made a silent vow to pay more attention to the company's finances, and began wondering if there wasn't some way she *could* lure the Renfrow's account away from the competition.

When Malcolm Halsey came on the line, his tone was guarded. "I assume this telephone line is secure, Mrs. Stark?"

"Yes."

"Good. I've spoken with my contact as you requested, and our mutual friend definitely has cause to be concerned. Something very hush-hush is afoot. If I were you, I would advise him of that."

Joanna sat down in her chair, gripping the receiver harder. "Who's behind it?"

"A gentleman with whom you have had . . . your differences in the past. He has placed an order for the merchandise we discussed earlier."

"When is he planning to take delivery? Tonight?"

"Oddly enough, sometime after eight tomorrow morning."

Six hours before the sale was to begin. Eight . . . it probably had to do with when the security personnel were due to change shifts—which meant one of them had sold out.

"Do you have any other particulars?" she asked.

Halsey chuckled—rare for a man with so little sense of humor. "Mrs. Stark, the ones I've just passed along were as difficult to mine as diamonds."

"Well, I thank you."

"You're very welcome. As I explained before, I don't know why I continue to assist you, but I'm likely to do so until the day I die. Perhaps you'll stop in again and let me know the outcome of all this? I should be most delighted to have a firsthand account. There is always a bottle of wine on ice for you."

ELEVEN

THE NEW APIA was the only Samoan-theme bar in the Chinatown area, perhaps in the entire city—and at that the motif only extended to the neon palm trees on its sign and the tropical caricatures on the cocktail napkins. Its proprietor, Rex Malauulu, had come to San Francisco in the mid-fifties, his life's savings of $500 tucked into an extra-large moneybelt, dreams of making his fortune on the mainland firmly planted in his mind. Within a dozen years he'd done just that—by his standards, anyway. Working at odd jobs, managing an apartment building in exchange for free rent, he'd saved every cent he could. Then he bought a small food concession, selling sandwiches from a truck to office workers. Next came the hole-in-the-wall hotdog stand, the vending machines, the take-out chicken place. Finally Rex realized his ultimate dream: the New Apia.

By 1970 when Joanna had answered the ad for a cheap studio apartment up the hill from Chinatown, Rex owned not only the bar but the building; he and his Swedish wife Loni plus several oddly assorted tenants inhabited the upper floors. Joanna and the gigantic man with curly black hair and a deceptively indolent way of moving had hit it off instantly; it helped that she was familiar with the Samoan capital—had actually been stranded there due to an odd set of circumstances on her recent journey from Manila to the States. Rex must have sensed the desperation behind the assured facade she'd tried to present, because he rented her the studio without checking her credit references or requiring a deposit, and he didn't cash her first check until she'd joyfully told him about landing the job at SSI.

Nineteen years had passed; Joanna was now Rex's long-est-standing tenant. For various reasons she'd kept the apartment even after her marriage; since she'd moved to Sonoma, she'd continued to pay the yearly rental, though she stayed there very seldom. Since her return from England, she hadn't set foot in it.

The phone service had been disconnected for years; there was nowhere to make the evening's necessary calls but the booth in the bar. As usual Rex stood behind the plank, clad in a voluminous apron and garish Hawaiian shirt, a Forty-niners cap covering the bald spot on the crown of his head. Joanna slipped through the door and set her overnight bag down, hoping to get into the booth before he spotted her.

"Hey, Jo!" Rex called. "You're back. Loni and me, we'd about given up on you."

"Hi, Rex." She kept going toward the booth.

"Come have a welcome-home drink—on me." Free drinks were dispensed at the New Apia for the most insignificant of reasons; Joanna had once known Rex to celebrate a customer's new gold filling.

She said, "Let me make a couple of phone calls first," and stepped into the booth. When she reached Adam Hawthorne's office, his secretary told her—as she had twice in the past hour—that he was in conference and could be disturbed under no circumstances. Joanna repeated that it was urgent she speak with him, and updated the number to the New Apia's.

Damn Adam's never-ending conference! she thought. Immediate steps needed to be taken to prevent the theft of the Van Gogh. She could go to the police, but they weren't likely to believe a tale based on unverifiable rumor. Besides, it was infinitely preferable to talk with Adam and let him bring his security firm in on it. The San Francisco Police Department had no art squad; their regular burglary details would not approach this potential crime the way specialists—such as those at New Scotland Yard—would.

Merely apprehending the inside man and the burglar was not enough; those dedicated to putting the brakes on art theft knew that such small arrests were only token gestures. But nabbing both the broker and the collector—*that* was the way to show those who sought illicitly acquired masterpieces that they were not invulnerable!

The air in the booth was hot and stuffy. Joanna opened its door and found the atmosphere outside not much better—cooler, but smoky. After a moment of indecision, she dropped another quarter into the slot and placed a credit card call to her home number. Again the phone rang fifteen times without an answer. Next she called Sally Jane. No answer there, either.

Before she left the booth, Joanna looked at her watch. Five to seven. She could try to call Tony Capello, but she'd given him the number here at the bar and knew he would phone if he found out anything worth reporting. When she slid onto the barstool in front of Rex, she asked, "Have I had any calls?"

"Calls? I didn't even know you were still alive. What'll you have?"

"White wine. No, make that a vodka tonic."

Rex nodded and moved down the bar. Joanna shoved a basket of moldy-looking popcorn away from her. The old woman to her right grunted disgustedly and pushed it farther along, in front of the empty stool beside her. It was Joanna's theory that the popcorn was the same stuff that had been put out when Rex opened the bar in 1967.

The New Apia was one of the few places she knew where nothing ever changed. It catered to a stable and fairly homogeneous clientele: all old, genteelly poor, dressed with a formality that included strange hats. The woman on her right had on what Joanna—whose generation had been raised hatless—supposed could be called a snood, made of beaded mesh, covering her white coif like a fancy hairnet. Three stools beyond her sat a man in a bowler, then a woman who looked as if a peacock had taken roost on her head, and finally another woman in a red contraption with a sequined veil that covered her face to her nose.

For years Joanna had wondered about the proliferation of eccentric headgear at the New Apia, but recently she'd concluded—partly from watching old movies on TV—that the hats had not seemed so strange during the era when they were purchased. Now they had become psychologically important to the old people in reduced circumstances who wore them: last symbols of a better time when these same men and women had lived in nice homes, had hired help, and dressed up to go out to far better establishments than a shabby neighborhood tavern. To give them up, no matter how closely they verged on the ridiculous by today's standards, would be to relinquish one's self-respect, hope, and—ultimately—one's hold on life. Once she realized that, Joanna had come to admire the old people's tenacity and courage.

Rex brought her drink. He toasted her with his beer mug and said, "Been a while."

"Yes. How're you doing?"

"Real good." As he spoke, he looked faintly surprised. Rex was a man who didn't spend much time thinking about the quality of his life, because he was always too busy looking out for others.

"And Loni?"

"Not so good. Her arthritis is getting worse all the time."

Loni had been an attractive, energetic woman when Joanna first knew her, but for many years now she had hardly ventured out of the Malauulus' second-floor apartment, preferring to spend her time behind drawn draperies, playing treacly fifties records on the stereo. Joanna suspected Loni's problem was more alcohol-related than arthritic, but she always listened sympathetically to Rex's reports of her aches and pains.

"That's too bad," she said.

Rex nodded lugubriously and went to serve a new arrival.

Suddenly the atmosphere in the bar seemed oppressive to Joanna. The old people might die off, but others replaced them. Loni might drink more and go out less, but Rex would still call it arthritis. The upstairs tenants might come and go, but they were still the same down-on-their-luck strays who accepted Rex's aid and comfort, then turned their backs on him as soon as things looked better. The lack of change, which for years had been reassuring to Joanna, now merely seemed depressing.

When Rex passed by she said, "Do you mind if I take my drink up to my apartment? There're some things I've got to do."

"Sure. You'll probably forget to bring the glass back down, but at least I'll know where to find it."

She retrieved her overnight bag and went outside. The night was clear and warm for San Francisco; people strolled by, and down the hill the sidewalks of Chinatown were crowded. Joanna fumbled for her keys and unlocked the street door to the apartments, then climbed two flights of creaky stairs to the third floor. Cooking smells hung in the hall—garlic and oregano tonight. Her own studio smelled of dry rot and dust. She snapped on the bulb in the paper-lantern shade, crossed the room, and set her bag and overnight case on the sofa bed. Then she took a long critical look around.

What she saw was a cramped dingy space full of items she'd bought long ago at flea markets and garage sales. The Oriental rug was threadbare; the white enamel of the bureau was chipped and cracked; the copper tea kettle on the two-burner stove in the pullman kitchen was stained and tarnished. Everything—even the crystal atomizer that had belonged to her mother and the silver-framed photograph of her with her parents—seemed to belong to someone else, an acquaintance, perhaps, who had years ago drifted out of her life. It was the first time she'd had such a reaction to the apartment.

When she'd first lived there she'd been miserable—a stranger in a city where all the doors seemed closed to her, including that of the house where her own son lived. Later, during her affair with David, she complained about the drawbacks of the place but had no real desire to move elsewhere. In all the years she'd hung onto it, the apartment had served as a sort of grounding wire that kept her connected to who Joanna Scherer Stark really was. But now she found she could no longer empathize with the lonely woman with the disreputable past who had inhabited these four walls—wasn't all that sure she would like her could they meet.

She kicked off her shoes and sat down on the sofa with her drink, trying to pinpoint the reason for this new reaction. True, she hadn't come to the apartment for well over a year, but the elapsed time didn't fully explain it. She'd once stayed away for three years, and when she'd finally returned it had been as much of a homecoming as the one she always experienced at SSI.

Why, then?

Well, for one thing, she'd changed radically in the past twelve months. She'd set out for London brashly self-confident and returned shaken to the core. Her resulting self-imposed isolation had forced her to spend time confronting all the insecurities and fears that she might have been able to dismiss had she merely been going about her business. A few days ago she would not have thought that she'd emerged stronger for it, but she had, and now a sense of change hung over her.

Maybe, she thought, it was time to get rid of the apartment. Her partnership in SSI necessitated her having a place here in the city, but she could certainly afford something better—something that didn't depress her, where she could take clients and friends.

She sipped her drink, thought about that some more, and felt a stirring of excitement. A house was impractical—too much upkeep for a largely absentee owner—but what about a condominium? For a long time the market had been depressed due to overbuilding, but she'd read that it was booming again. If you bought into one of the new buildings early, you could specify certain things you wanted, even floorplans....

All right, she told herself, here's what you do. Finish off this Parducci business, because that's the only real obstacle to starting a new life. When that's over, tell Rex you're giving up this place. God knows he'll probably be delighted, since he can get several hundred dollars more than he's charging. Take Mom's atomizer and the family photo, because you can't completely shed the people who gave birth to you and formed you. But leave the rest of it. Get yourself a place you like and start to put some real effort into SSI. You've always worked, don't really feel comfortable without it, and that firm could be a top outfit if you set your mind to it. I bet you could get the Renfrow's account, because their current security people have fucked up royally...

And then she realized it was time to call Adam Hawthorne again. Past time. In order to prevent the planned theft they needed to get moving. If the secretary gave her any of that conference stuff this time, she'd go over there and bully her way into the meeting.

She stood up and started downstairs, fulfilling Rex's prophesy by leaving his glass on the kitchen counter.

TWELVE

AT THREE-THIRTY the next morning Joanna sat in the conference room at Renfrow's with Adam, Mike Jacobson of Jacobson Security, and Lieutenant John Brady of the SFPD burglary detail. She had forced her way into Adam's meeting at a little before nine; it had taken an hour for Adam to contact Jacobson, and more than that for Jacobson to convince Brady that the threat to the Van Gogh was serious enough that he should attend to it himself, rather than sending one of his subordinates. Mapping out a strategy for dealing with the guards on the midnight-to-eight shift had taken even longer. Now they were in the process of talking with each of them. So far none had acted in a manner that indicated complicity.

Joanna got up, stretched, and went to pour herself some more coffee. She held the pot up questioningly at the others. Adam shook his head and rubbed his eyes; Brady also declined; Jacobson held his cup out eagerly. She filled it, smiling faintly at the incongruity between the four of them and their surroundings. The room was paneled in rosewood, its walls covered by original lithographs and leatherbound volumes in glass-fronted bookcases. The carpet was a Sarouk; the pedestal table and chairs were Sheraton; the sterling silver coffee service on the matching sideboard was turn of the century; the cups and saucers were Wedgwood.

And around the table were seated an auction house owner whose Brooklyn accent grew thicker with the passing hours; an Irish cop whose appearance bordered on the stereotypical; a black security specialist who had once played pro basketball; and a woman with a civilized facade and a past that would raise the eyebrows of all three men. Their discussion of how to trap the potential thief suited the room even less than they themselves did.

As she set down the coffeepot, Joanna became aware of Adam's gaze. In a voice edged with sarcasm he said, "Something's funny, toots?"

She sobered quickly and shook her head. Time was growing short, and so were tempers. Whimsical irony was inappropriate now.

Mike Jacobson flipped a page on the clipboard in front of him. "Three down, two to go," he said. "What'd you think of the last one, Lieutenant?"

Brady rubbed his stubbled chin. "Didn't react to you saying you wanted to change his station. Looked glad the next shift was coming on early, just like the other two."

"Could be our guy's a good actor."

"Could be Mrs. Stark's information is wrong."

"My contact is extremely reliable, Lieutenant," she said.

Brady continued speaking to Jacobson as if she were not in the room. "Her other contact—Capello—claims to have found out nothing."

She had called Tony Capello while they were waiting for Brady to arrive. He told her he'd talked to a number of people, all of whom said she must be out of her mind. "Nobody's gonna try to pull off a job like that," he concluded. "You owe me fifty bucks, but if you promise to stay away from me from now on, you can just keep it."

Now she said, "Capello's a crook. He doesn't want to get involved."

Brady sighed and looked at the ceiling.

Mike Jacobson flashed her a sympathetic smile; the lieutenant had been curt with him the whole time, too. An outsider might have assumed Brady's attitude was based in both racism and sexism; Joanna and Mike knew it had its roots in the cop's traditional scorn for private security personnel.

Adam said, "It's possible Mrs. Stark may have received false information, but we've got too much at risk not to follow up on it."

Brady hesitated, then looked at Jacobson. "Who's up at bat next?"

"Name's Pete Gulevich. Age twenty-six. Been with us three years. Dependable, smart. One of our top men."

"Yeah," Brady said wearily, "you already told us—twice—that you only put top men on this job."

Jacobson tapped the eraser end of his pencil on the table, looking as if he was about to make a sharp retort. Then he cleared his throat and went on, "Gulevich just got married, has a kid on the way. He's looking to move up in the company, knows he's got a future with us. He—"

"Can we skip the sales pitch and get him in here?"

The silence that followed Brady's remark was tense. Joanna could see Jacobson's jaw bulge as he clenched his teeth. Adam said quickly, "I appreciate Mike giving us the background on his men. It helps me to know what to look for when they come in here."

Brady shrugged.

Adam asked, "Mike, what were you about to say?"

"I was about to say that Gulevich volunteered for this assignment—in spite of being newly married and having a regular day shift that's more convenient to his home. He bears watching."

If Brady felt he'd been put in his place, his expression failed to reveal it.

Jacobson went to the door to call the guard in. Joanna glanced at Adam; he winked at her. During the past hours, her respect for him had grown greatly: Faced with a potentially ruinous situation, he'd remained calm and tactful, smoothing over hurt feelings and defusing arguments. It was a side of her often abrasive friend that she'd never seen.

Gulevich was a slender young man, sallow faced, with dishwater blond hair. As he entered the room he walked aggressively, bouncing slightly on the balls of his feet. His blue eyes were sharp and analytical as they surveyed the gathering before him. Very much a man on the way up, Joanna thought. Or on the make.

Jacobson said to him, "You know Mr. Hawthorne, Pete. The others are Mrs. Stark and Mr. Brady—colleagues of mine."

After a moment's hesitation Gulevich nodded at Joanna and Brady. To Jacobson he said, "Is everything okay, sir? I mean, you sent Mills to relieve me."

"Everything's fine, Pete. Sit down, please." Jacobson gestured at one of the deceptively fragile-looking chairs.

Gulevich eyed it dubiously, then sat.

Jacobson remained standing. "This meeting concerns a shift in scheduling. I take it nothing unusual has occurred tonight?"

"I'd have reported it if it had, sir."

"Nothing out of the ordinary at all?"

"No, sir. Why, is something—?"

"I'll ask the questions, Gulevich."

A trace of wariness showed in the guard's expression. His posture straightened ever so slightly.

"Now—" Jacobson began.

As when they'd questioned the other personnel, Brady interrupted. "I'd like to ask Mr. Gulevich some questions, Mike."

"Go ahead."

"Mr. Gulevich, I understand you're one of the up-and-coming young men at Jacobson Security."

"Well, I like to think—"

"And that your co-workers have a high regard for you."

"We get on. Not that I have much in common with—"

"But they trust you."

"Sure."

"And they talk freely with you—on coffee breaks and so forth?"

"Well . . . yeah."

"What kinds of things do you talk about?"

"Well, just . . . our families, sports, what we're going to do on our days off. You know."

"So the atmosphere is pretty relaxed?"

"Sure."

"Relaxed enough that somebody might let something slip that they wouldn't ordinarily tell you?"

"I . . . well, I don't know. I mean, what wouldn't they want me to know?"

Joanna took up the questioning. "Let's back up a minute, Mr. Gulevich. Do you also talk about work on your breaks?"

"Of course."

"Have you talked about the Van Gogh?"

"Ma'am?"

"Have you talked about the painting? And the upcoming auction?"

Gulevich wet his lips. "Not all that much."

"Oh, come on, Mr. Gulevich. You're guarding a painting that's expected to bring some sixty million dollars at auction, and you haven't *talked* about it?"

"Well, we've talked about it, sure. I mean, when you've got this piece of canvas with some flowers on it that somebody's gonna pay more than all of us put together will ever see—"

"Did you ever talk about someone stealing it?"

The guard's pupils dilated; his tongue darted out and touched his lips again. "Ma'am!"

"Don't look so shocked, Mr. Gulevich. It's only natural that you people would speculate about that."

". . . I guess."

"Think back over the last few days. Do you remember anyone talking about an attempt to steal the painting—no matter how hypothetically?"

Gulevich closed his eyes in a bad imitation of deep thought. When he opened them again they were wide and guileless, but there was a pinpoint of something that could either be fear or anger in their centers. "Ma'am," he said, "I honestly don't remember anything like that."

"That's too bad, because there *is* going to be an attempt to steal it—around the time your shift's supposed to end this morning."

The guard's forehead looked damp now. He turned to Jacobson. "Sir, is that true?"

Jacobson nodded.

Adam said, "That's the reason for the change in scheduling Mr. Jacobson mentioned earlier. We have reason to believe someone on the inside is assisting the thief. So we're shifting everyone's work station. From now on you'll be upstairs at the front, where Geddes is."

Gulevich's eyes darted back to Jacobson. "Sir, Geddes isn't too bright. I don't think he should have my station. I'm at the back door, it's a vulnerable—"

"Leave the work assignments to us, Gulevich."

"But—"

"In addition, we're rotating the shifts early," Adam went on. "The eight o'clock has been notified to come on at six."

"Six!" His head swiveled back toward his employer.

"Yes, Gulevich?" Jacobson said.

"I was just going to say that . . . well, to volunteer to stay on and help out. If somebody's really trying to steal that painting, you'll be needing more men, and I'd be glad—"

"Thank you, but it won't be necessary. Without the inside man, there will be minimal risk."

"The inside—" he looked down at his hands; their fingers pressed hard against his thighs. When he looked up, it was directly at Joanna. "Ma'am, what you were saying about the guys talking on break?"

"Yes?"

"Well, the other day when I was in the office picking up my paycheck, there was one of the guys . . . I don't know his name, but I'm pretty sure he's on the shift that comes on after mine . . . and he was talking . . . well, now that I know somebody's planning to rip off the painting, what he said made sense."

Joanna had to admire Gulevich; he was not only tenacious, but inventive. "What did he say?"

"Something about that Van Gogh, and how Renfrow's was gonna be out a pile of money. I can't remember it all. I'm sorry." He hung his head, then looked up, face suffused with fresh hope. "Listen, what I can do is stay on shift and get the guy talking again. I can make him tell me—"

"I'd rather *you* told *us*."

Gulevich sat very still.

"Tell us about the arrangements, Pete," she added.

"I don't know about any arrangements!"

"You *do*, dammit! Tell us—*now*, before it's too late!"

He stared at her, then looked at each of the others. What he saw in their faces made his shoulders sag. His head drooped forward, and he kneaded his thighs with his hands. After a moment he began to speak in a shaky voice, telling them what they needed to know.

THIRTEEN

"GOD," JOANNA SAID to Adam, "by the time Brady took him out of here, I was actually beginning to feel sorry for the poor guy."

"I know what you mean." Adam slumped in his chair, rubbing at his eyes. "Gulevich is really one of the would-be's of the world."

"The—?"

"What I call the ones who want it all but never achieve any of it. They've got big plans—become a superstar, beat the system at Las Vegas, write the big best-seller, make a fortune on the stock market. But they haven't got what it takes. Something's missing in them—whether it's talent or smarts or discipline or just plain pizzazz. And when they fail, they spend the rest of their lives with their noses pressed to the glass, wondering why they're outside while the rest of us are inside. In a way they're sadder cases than the total fuck-ups, because they come just close enough to get a taste of what they're missing."

Joanna nodded, thinking about Pete Gulevich. He could have gone far at Jacobson Security, but instead he and a friend who trained racehorses had concocted a scheme to build their own stable by purchasing a good horse and participating in the cheap claiming races. Gulevich had been so impressed by his friend's self-proclaimed expertise and so eager to finance his share of the stake that he'd allowed himself to be talked into helping steal the Van Gogh by a stranger who had approached him through the bartender at his neighborhood tavern.

"How did he ever expect to get away with it?" she said.

Adam shrugged. "Probably thought he could bluff his way out, or pin it on somebody else. Or maybe he just didn't think that far ahead. You want some more coffee?"

"Yes, please."

He got up and took the coffeepot to the door, where he spoke with someone outside. It was only a little after seven, but already the auction house hummed with activity. The police were there, of course, waiting until it was time for a now cooperative Gulevich to hand out a dummy painting to his accomplice. The closed-circuit TV crew had arrived perhaps fifteen minutes ago and begun laying cable for the sale; another crew was moving furniture. In spite of having had very little sleep in the past forty-eight hours, Joanna felt energized, both by the undercurrent of excitement here at Renfrow's and the prospect of Antony Parducci being caught in a police trap.

When Adam returned with the full coffeepot, she held out her cup and said, "Are Brady and Jacobson sure Gulevich will cooperate?"

"He's got no choice. But if he's got any wild ideas about tipping off his accomplice, Brady'll handle him. Brady's kind of an asshole, but I sense he's a good cop."

"He'd better be. If everything goes smoothly on this end, the burglary detail'll have a clear shot at Parducci, maybe the collector, too. I just hope they don't content themselves with grabbing Parducci and letting his client go."

"Well, we should know in a few hours."

Joanna set her coffee cup down and stretched her arms over her head. "I ought to go back to my apartment before anything happens," she said. "I need to change my clothes for the auction."

"Why? What you've got on is fine."

She glanced down at her short black skirt. It was barely rumpled, and the longish turquoise jacket that hung over the back of her chair would hide any wrinkles in her cream-colored blouse. While others in the front rows might flaunt furs and diamonds, that wasn't her style. She didn't even own a fur, and her diamonds—a bracelet and earrings that David had given her as a wedding present—spent more time in the safe-deposit box than anywhere else.

"I'll stay," she said.

The minutes ticked by in companionable silence. Adam read the morning paper, grumbling frequently about politicians, the economy, the high crime rate, and the stupid people who write to Dear Abby. He didn't much like Abby's replies, either: "All she ever says is 'see a counselor.' Anybody can tell you that." When Joanna got herself a second cup of coffee, he looked censoriously at her over the reading glasses he'd donned with considerable embarrassment. "You shouldn't drink so much of that," he said. "You want to get heart palpitations?"

She made a face at him and sat down, kicking off her shoes and propping her feet on another chair. Adam disappeared behind the sports section, mumbling something about greedy athletes.

Joanna wiggled her stockinged toes and sipped the fresh French roast. She ought to be nervous, she knew, keyed up over Parducci's imminent apprehension. But instead she felt almost serene. Why?

Behind the paper Adam said, "Poor baby—they wouldn't give him one point five million to play ball. I wish *I* could hold out for one point five million instead of working my ass off."

Joanna smiled, realizing the source of her sense of well-being, David had also been a morning grumbler—the kind who could encounter any number of irritations merely on his way to get the paper from the front walk. There had been many mornings when she'd awakened in a cheery mood, soon to find that the only cheerfulness left was that with which she could have killed him. But once he was gone, the very first of all the many things she'd missed throughout the lonely days was David's grumpiness. It had been as much a part of their (usually) happy life together as good sex, one of those small indicators built into a successful marriage that tells the partners everything is copacetic: *David's bitching about Reagan again—all's right with the world.*

She laughed aloud at the memory. And at the realization that Adam was something of a curmudgeon, too.

He lowered the paper and peered over it, pushing his reading glasses down onto the bridge of his nose. "Well, aren't you the chipper one, toots."

"Can't help it."

"I take it your good mood has to do with Parducci being about to get tossed in the slammer?"

"Something like that."

Adam folded the sports section, skimmed it onto the table. "You almost caught him once yourself, didn't you— after that mess at the de Young?"

"Yes."

"I guess after coming that close, his arrest takes on a personal meaning for you."

She hesitated. While she was beginning to like Adam a lot, to feel more of a connection than mere physical attraction, she wasn't prepared to trust him wholly. She'd been hurt badly, and recently had made what she considered an excessive number of mistakes where the opposite sex was concerned. Still, she didn't want to cut him off with one of her stock answers or, worse, to lie.

She said, "Someday, maybe, I'll tell you more about Antony Parducci and me."

Surprise and curiosity flickered in Adam's eyes, but he merely said, "I'd like that. And I'll wait eagerly."

Their eyes met and held, but before either could speak again, the door opened. The man who entered was tall and heavy, with gray blond hair and a handsome face that was bloated by recent though not habitual dissipation. With a shock Joanna recognized Jerome Eckridge. He had aged out of proportion to the time elapsed since they'd last met.

"What the hell are the police doing here?" he demanded.

Adam stood. "Jerry, I didn't expect you this early."

"Never mind that—I want to know what's going on. There's a cop in the hall—Brady. I know him from when he handled a burglary at my Seacliff place."

"It's nothing to worry about—"

"The hell you say! What's happened to my painting?"

"The painting's right where it should be. Brady's just—"

"Brady's their top man on burglary. I know because I insisted on him when the Seacliff house was broken into. He doesn't come out on routine calls."

"Jerry, will you please sit down! Have some coffee. Joanna, will you ask somebody to bring a clean cup?"

"I don't want any coffee." Then Eckridge looked at Joanna, as if he hadn't noticed until then that there was someone else in the room. "Joanna Stark. I haven't seen you in years. What're you . . . wait a minute—you own a security firm!"

"Jerry, sit!" Adam pointed at one of the chairs.

Eckridge did as he was told. His face had gone pale, and he looked sick.

"Now," Adam said, "I will repeat—there is *nothing* wrong. Joanna came across some information yesterday that led us to think we might have a security breach, but it's taken care of. Brady's seeing to that."

Eckridge looked sicker. "Anything happens to that painting, and my whole life goes down the toilet."

"It won't—I guarantee it. Now how about that coffee?"

Eckridge nodded unenthusiastically, and Adam went to fetch a cup.

Joanna said, "He's telling the truth, Jerry. Everything really is under control."

He sighed, leaning back heavily. "Then I guess I have you to thank for it. Sure been a long time, hasn't it? Where've you been keeping yourself?"

"Sonoma. I moved up there after David died and renovated an old farmhouse."

"That so. I've been staying off and on at my place near Glen Ellen."

"I'd forgotten—you have a ranch there."

"For the moment I do. It's being sold. You heard about my divorce, and the takeover attempt?"

"Yes. I'm sorry."

"You're one of the few. Most people say I brought it on myself. Maybe I did, I don't know."

Adam should have returned by now. Joanna looked at her watch, saw it was a few minutes after eight. Had something gone wrong with the handoff of the dummy painting?

She said, "Tell me about the Van Gogh. It's one of his works that I'm unfamiliar with. You've had it a long time?"

"Around twenty-five years. It was the cornerstone of my collection. Funny how that happened." Eckridge smiled wryly. "At the time I bought the Glen Ellen place I gave a good bit of thought to community property. There was a clause in my prenuptial agreement with Sandra that was designed to prevent her family's art collection from falling into my hands, should she decide to share her inheritance with me. The clause was reciprocal: Any artworks I acquired after the marriage would be my separate property. So I heard about this Van Gogh that could be had cheaply, and became an art collector in order to protect some of my capital. Ironically, it became a passionate avocation."

"Where did you hear about the painting?"

Eckridge twisted around, looking at the door. "Where the hell is Adam with that cup?"

"He probably got waylaid by one of the work crews. There're a million things to be done yet. About the Van Gogh—"

"I don't want to talk about it. It hurts to give it up."
Eckridge stood. "I'm going to get some breakfast. You can
join me if you stay off the subject of the auction."

"I think I'll wait here. I need to talk to Adam about his
security; I'm hoping he might throw the contract my firm's
way."

"Suit yourself."

As Eckridge went out, Joanna wondered about his reluc-
tance to talk about the Van Gogh. Was it simply because
after that afternoon it would no longer be his, or was there
something more? Adam had said its provenance, prior to
Jerry's ownership, was hazy....

In a few minutes Adam returned, trailed by Mike Jacobson. "Where's Jerry?" he asked, setting down the clean cup.

"He decided to get some breakfast."

"Good. I don't want him buzzing around here. He'd only
get in the way."

"Why do you suppose he wants to be here anyway?"

Adam shrugged. "Maybe he thinks his presence will
magically ensure him getting the price he needs. Maybe he's
a masochist. Who knows?"

"Did the handoff go as planned?"

Jacobson nodded. "Like clockwork. Gulevich is now
being escorted to the Hall of Justice, and Brady's men are
tailing the fellow with our package." Jacobson's satisfaction was grim; he obviously knew that the breach of security would lose him the Renfrow's account.

It was to Adam's credit that he didn't go into that in front
of Joanna. He merely poured Jacobson coffee and pointed
out the copy of the *Chronicle*. Mike buried his nose in the
sports pages, and Adam said to Joanna, "You play gin
rummy?"

"Yes."

"Good." He fetched cards and they sat down at the end
of the pedestal table. Adam was a good player, but dis-
tracted; she was some sixty points up on him when Brady

returned at a little after ten. What he had to tell them sent Joanna's spirits plummeting.

The thief, a young Latino named Hector Morales, had been tailed to a coffee shop near Kaiser Hospital on Geary Boulevard, where he waited in the parking lot for close to an hour. He appeared to be expecting someone to meet him, but finally left and drove across town to Islais Creek Resort. He took the package containing the dummy painting inside, and he and Tony Capello were just opening it when the police entered and arrested them.

It explained why Capello had been so adamant that nothing was going down at Renfrow's: He was the fagin who had arranged the job.

What it didn't explain was why Antony Parducci hadn't kept his rendezvous with Morales—and where he was right now.

FOURTEEN

THE HALL where the auction was to be held was hushed, and nearly full. People still filed in on the deep-piled runners, but as soon as they came through the door they lowered their voices, entering into the spirit of quiet decorum. Clothing rustled, people coughed discreetly, but if they spoke they did so in whispers. A great deal of money was about to change hands, and most of the attendees respected money above all else.

Flowers along the Rhone stood under near-perfect lighting on an easel on the dais: a smallish canvas—perhaps eighteen inches on a side—executed in the swirling brushstrokes and thick impasto that marked the works of Van Gogh's last years. The colors were more subdued than the brilliant yellows of the celebrated *Sunflowers*: blues and aquamarines, with only highlights of golds and pinks and reds. The dynamic composition was what made it special: slashes of paint that rendered the flowers fresh and alive nearly a hundred years after their creation.

Special, yes. But some sixty million dollars' worth of special? Joanna thought not.

She occupied a place of honor in the first row of the gilt and velvet chairs that the furniture rental company had trucked in that morning. The others at the front of the room represented the cream of the international art world: prominent dealers and museum curators; wealthy and serious collectors; sharp-eyed men and women who served as representatives both for commercial concerns and for collectors who preferred to keep their names and faces out of the papers. There was also a smattering of socialites and celebrities—people who were not expected to bid, but whose presence was thought to add "tone." The fashionable woman to Joanna's right was one of these. Lesley Sheppard's late husband had been one of David's multimillionaire clients. Lesley expressed pleasure at seeing Joanna and planted a little social kiss on her cheek, but she had to make an obvious effort to conceal both surprise and chagrin that David Stark's upstart widow commanded such an important seat at this event.

The platform where the easel stood was raised three steps above the rest of the hall. To one side two members of the fine-arts sales department sat at a table, prepared to accept telephone bids. Auctioneer Hugh Willoughby stood behind them, soberly clad as if this were a funeral, seemingly relaxed but—as Joanna knew from having spoken to him in the hallway fifteen minutes earlier—as tightly wound as a child's toy top. Willoughby was one of the foremost auctioneers in the business, a Canadian by birth who had drifted south after the Second World War and taken up museum work. In the early seventies he had gone to work for Butterfield's, and had become known for a low-key style and refined but insistent salesmanship. Over the years his deceptively easy manner had lulled many a patron into parting with far more than he or she had envisioned. Adam credited Willoughby's joining the Renfrow staff four years ago with much of the firm's recent growth.

Joanna glanced toward the rear of the room, searching for Adam. When she'd last seen him, he and Jerry Eckridge had been closeted in the conference room near one of the closed-circuit TV monitors. Adam hoped to take a seat in the back of the hall when the bidding opened, but Eckridge was in such a nervous state that he needed continual reassurance. Whether Adam would be able to leave him alone for the duration of the auction remained to be seen.

At exactly two o'clock Hugh Willoughby stepped to the podium and cleared his throat. This latter was totally unnecessary; the patrons sat attentive and alert. Joanna glanced toward the rear once more and saw Adam slip through the door and into a chair on the aisle.

"Good afternoon, ladies and gentlemen," Willoughby said. "I don't think I need to tell you what a historic event this sale is, nor do I need to extol the virtues of our offering." He extended a hand toward the easel beside him. "We all know the work of Vincent Van Gogh, and we all are able to see what a fine example of his genius we have before us."

He paused, looking at the assemblage. Joanna knew he was making note of the locations of those who would be bidding, fixing in his mind the individual signals they would use.

After a moment he continued. "The successful bidder for this painting will become the owner of an important piece of the world's artistic heritage. *Flowers along the Rhone* represents the zenith of Van Gogh's talent. It was painted at the peak of his productivity, during a respite from the madness that plagued him, when he was at peace and able to meld the elements of his style into a cohesive, mature whole. That is what makes this work exceptional."

Willoughby smiled wryly, almost confessionally, in a manner that made Joanna feel he was sharing a private joke with her and her alone. She knew he was establishing similar rapport with every person in the hall; even the most hard-bitten of professionals had been known to fall for Hugh's self-effacing demeanor.

"But there I go again," he said, "doing just what I said there was no need to. The painting somehow commands a tribute." He turned slightly toward the easel—but not for long enough to make the crowd restless. When he faced them again, he was all business.

"We will begin now," he said. "An opening bid of seventeen million has been requested. We will open with the leading mail bid of twenty million. I will now entertain others, in increments of one million dollars, please."

A man at the end of the second row, whom Joanna recognized as a dealer's representative, removed his glasses. Had she not been schooled by attendance at many previous auctions, she would not have noticed the gesture, much less recognized it as a signal for a bid.

Willoughby nodded. "I have twenty-one million."

The sales representatives had picked up their telephone receivers. In the interest of decorum, the bells had been stilled, but Joanna could see the lights of the multiple lines flashing. Both representatives signaled Willoughby.

"I have twenty-two million. Twenty-three million."

Joanna felt someone behind her make a slight motion.

"Twenty-four million."

A French dealer she knew crossed his legs. The curator of a well-endowed eastern museum smoothed one of her eyebrows. The bid kept climbing, past thirty million.

Telephone calls continued to come in. Some bids were entered, then topped by nearly invisible signals from people in the hall. A young woman two seats away from Joanna pushed the bid to forty-four million by crossing her arms. The man with the glasses stayed in the running; whoever had been bidding behind Joanna remained still. A flurry of bids advanced the price to fifty million, which was immediately bettered by the young woman.

The atmosphere in the hall grew tense; a rough current flowed under the surface of the genteel proceedings. The bids came faster. Willoughby worked the crowd, timing his responses more quickly to give the patrons less time to think. Joanna found herself pressing damp palms together when a phone call advanced the bid to sixty million.

The French dealer advanced to sixty-one. The man in the glasses topped it. The young woman immediately folded her arms.

Another phone bid: sixty-four million. For a moment the price hung there—a million dollars below what Adam had predicted the painting would go for.

Willoughby fingered a small ivory stick—a nineteenth
century netsuke that Renfrow's had substituted for the
cruder and largely out-of-favor hammer.

The man in the second row removed his glasses.

The woman folded her arms again.

The man responded.

"Sixty-seven million. Do I have an answering bid?"

The air in the hall felt electrically charged. Joanna found
she was breathing fast; her palms were drenched. Beside her,
she saw Lesley Sheppard's fingers press hard against her
silk-encased thigh.

Joanna glanced from one bidder to the other. From a few
rows back she wouldn't even have been able to tell they *were*
participating, but at this vantage she could see their eyes.
The man's were flat and expressionless. The woman's were
focused on the Van Gogh; then they moved calculatingly to
the auctioneer.

She folded her arms again.

Willoughby said, "I have sixty-eight million dollars. Is
there an answering bid?"

The man sat rigid.

Willoughby looked at the sales representatives. The lights
on the phones no longer flashed.

After a weighty pause Willoughby said, "I have a hammer price of sixty-eight million dollars." With great ceremony he held up the ivory stick and tapped on the edge of
the podium—once, twice, three times.

The sounds shattered the tension. People expelled their
breath, shifted in their chairs, murmured to one another.
Then from the rear came the sound of hands clapping. The
occupants of the front rows swiveled and craned their necks.
Joanna couldn't see who had started it, but suddenly she,
along with everyone else, was on her feet, bursting into
riotous applause. The fervent response was thoroughly
atypical, somewhat shocking, and extremely satisfying.

When Joanna looked for Adam, he was moving down the aisle, on his way to speak with Hugh Willoughby, stopping here and there to receive congratulatory handshakes. As he passed the front row, he winked at her and said, "That'll buy a hell of a lotta lentils!"

AFTERWARD THERE WAS a champagne reception in the outer sales room. Joanna wandered about, renewing some old acquaintances and listening to the speculative chatter that eddied around her. Not much was known about the successful bidder—who had left after a brief conference with Adam—except that she represented a consortium of investors. Less was known about the man who had bid against her, but several people thought he might have been there on behalf of a German industrialist. The number of phone bids was a subject of comment: Many said the last series had been made by a single persistent bidder. Intermixed with the guesswork and fledgling rumors was the usual talk of obscenely high art prices, but no one sounded particularly dismayed. In this sort of crowd, Joanna thought, being present when big money was spent was the next best thing to spending it oneself.

Adam, flushed with pride, champagne in hand, was kept busy accepting congratulations. Jerry Eckridge was not present, which made it easier for everyone to gossip about his financial and marital problems, the secret of the painting's ownership having leaked, as such secrets are wont to do. Finally Joanna refilled her glass and withdrew to an alcove from which she could observe the gathering through the fronds of a thick screening palm, and wonder how she had managed to live through innumerable similar ones during the nine years of her marriage.

After she had got over being intimidated by San Francisco's art-collecting elite, she had accepted its members and their social functions as a matter of course—unenthusiastic, but aware that this was her husband's world, peopled with his clients. David had shared her reservations about it to some degree; at times he would scoff at the conventions, rail at the pretentiousness. But he had also possessed an empathy that had enabled him to look beyond the people's veneers to the genuine human beings underneath.

Joanna supposed that if she cared enough, she would be able to view this crowd of convivial champagne drinkers in the same way David would have. But she didn't care, had changed too much to want to keep up the old ties. Being there simply depressed her in the same way the New Apia had, and she began to regret promising to have dinner with Adam. After all, wasn't he firmly rooted in this world, too?

She was trying to think of an excuse for cancelling when the palm fronds parted and Adam peered through them. "You hiding?"

"All this is getting to me."

"Me, too. Let's blow this joint."

"How can you—"

"They don't care whether I'm here or not, as long as the champagne keeps flowing." He reached around the palm and took her by the hand. "Let's go."

THE RESTAURANT was one of the old-line Italian places in North Beach that she knew by reputation but somehow had never visited. It was fairly early for a Saturday dinner—only six o'clock by the time they were able to escape Renfrow's—and they were shown immediately to an intimate private dining room on the second floor. By the time they'd been served an excellent white wine from Tuscany and presented with menus, Joanna realized she was starving. Lunch had consisted of sandwiches brought in from a nearby deli; she'd been too upset about Parducci eluding the police to eat much. Now she opened the menu and scanned it; everything looked wonderful.

"Have you eaten here before?" she asked Adam.

"Many times. It's Ligurian style—from the area around Genoa. Great pesto sauce."

"You order then—otherwise I'll just ask for one of everything."

He looked pleased and set his menu aside. Toasting with his wineglass, he said, "Here's to the free-spending Japanese."

"That's who the bidder represented then?"

"Yes—a Tokyo insurance company. They plan to establish a small museum of Impressionist and Post-Impressionist works, so at least *Flowers* will be available to the general public."

The waiter reappeared; he conferred with Adam and departed, smiling in approval of the choices.

Adam poured them both more wine. "You look kind of down."

"Don't mind me. It's the Parducci thing, that's all."

"Too bad about that. Wonder why he didn't show?"

"All I can figure is that he knew the police had been brought in. The man's uncanny when it comes to gathering information. But then, he wouldn't have survived so long as a top broker if he wasn't."

"Wasn't he presumed dead at one time?"

"For years, between the time he stopped pulling jobs on his own and became a broker, and when he arranged that abortive thing at the de Young."

"No, I mean recently. Wasn't he supposed to have drowned in England last year?"

"Yes, but I knew he hadn't."

"You had proof?"

"Not the kind the police would accept at face value."

A pasta course arrived—*trenette* with pesto sauce. Joanna found that not even the talk of Parducci could spoil her appetite. Between forkfuls of the ribbonlike noodles, she asked, "Did you get a chance to talk with Lieutenant Brady after the auction?"

"Yeah, I called him. The thief—Hector Morales—is claiming Capello simply asked him to pick up a package at Renfrow's. Capello's claiming the kid burst in with this package, talking about a big score. Neither will name anyone else."

"There would have to have been a middleman, someone besides Parducci. He would have been the one who contacted Capello, and probably Gulevich in that bar. If only Gulevich could tell us more about him—"

"Could, or *would*. Do you suppose it was the middleman who was to meet Morales in that parking lot?"

Joanna shook her head. "Not if I know the way Parducci operates. He trusts someone else with the arrangements, but he's always on hand for the delivery."

"You know that much about him?"

She busied herself with scraping the last bit of pesto sauce from her plate. "Everything I need to."

Adam left it at that. They were silent while the *burrida* was served. A robust Barolo came with it. Joanna sampled both the fish stew and the wine and decided they were too good to allow talk of Parducci to interfere with her enjoyment. She steered the conversation away from him, asking Adam about his decision to leave Brooklyn.

As they ate he told her of the antique store he had loved, and of the wife who had hated it; of how he had resisted her repeated urgings to go to work for one of her father's car dealerships; of how both the business and the marriage had gone into a tailspin. He came west, he said, with only the few thousand dollars he could salvage from the business; the rest he left to his wife. His own family had disowned him; they hadn't communicated in years.

During the salad course—mixed greens with eggs, anchovies, black olives and garlic—Joanna told him about how she had also run away from home, at nineteen, after her alcoholic mother had committed suicide. She had blamed her father, she said, because he was in love with someone else. Now she was thinking of reestablishing contact, but wasn't sure it was worth the effort. Maybe she was better off without a family. What did he think?

"I can't advise you on that, toots."

She set her fork down. "Adam, will you do me one favor?"

"Sure, what?"

"Don't call me 'toots.'"

He looked mildly surprised. "It's just what I call women I like. What do you want to be called?"

"By my name. What's wrong with Joanna?"

"Joanna, or Jo?"

"Everybody calls me Jo. Use the whole name. Please."

"Be glad to—toots."

After the salad she thought she couldn't eat another mouthful, but the stuffed peaches in white wine sauce *were* exceptional. Then espresso seemed a necessity, and they lingered over it. When they finally left the restaurant, the streets were fog cloaked, the spell of clear weather apparently having broken. It seemed natural, since they were so close, that she invite him to come see the New Apia and her apartment. She didn't take many people to either, but Adam would appreciate their perverse charm.

Rex was behind the bar as usual, looking somewhat melancholy. The elderly people sat in what seemed to be assigned places, nursing their drinks. Her landlord brightened when Joanna introduced him to Adam. She hadn't brought a man to the New Apia since she and David had first been together—Steve Rafferty had claimed it depressed him just to look through the door—and she could tell Rex was pleased. While they sat at the bar Adam chatted with him about the place; how long he had owned it, how much the building had appreciated since the sixties. Rex winked approvingly at Joanna before he went to serve a newcomer; it meant, she knew, that he considered Adam a "real regular guy."

Joanna said, "You cheered him up."

Adam shrugged and drank off the cheap wine Rex had poured on the house, not even grimacing. "People always feel better when they can talk about their successes."

"You should know—after today."

"I wonder. Maybe today wasn't such a good thing. It may have been my moment, as they say. What if there's never another?"

He'd spoken too seriously for her to discount the idea, but she had no answer for him. After a bit she said, "Let's go upstairs. I'll show you my pied-á-terre."

They were nearly to the door when Rex called, "Say, Jo— I nearly forgot. Did you know E.J.'s up there?"

Her son had taken to using the apartment during the past year for his infrequent trips into the city. Now, at least, she knew where he was. "When did he get here?"

"I ran into him when I was going up after closing last night. I think he's still there—leastways, I didn't see him leave."

She looked up at Adam. "I guess you're about to meet E.J."

His slightly disgruntled expression told her that an empty apartment had held a certain allure for him, but he wasn't at all sure about one occupied by an unfamiliar young man.

Joanna smiled. "Really, you'll like him."

They went to the street door and climbed the two creaking flights. The hallway was silent; the only sound was Eddie Fisher crooning downstairs in the Malauulus' apartment; no light showed under any of the doors.

"E.J. may have gone out," she said, fumbling with her keys.

"That doesn't mean he won't be back."

She inserted the key in the lock and paused, looking up at him. "What's wrong—is his presence interfering with plans you may have harbored?"

He gave her shoulder a playful shove. "Just open the door, will you?"

The temperature inside was colder than that in the hall, even though she remembered leaving the electric heater on the night before. She frowned and felt for the light switch. Snapped it on, blinked at the sudden glare.

The blue draperies at the window flapped, damp from the foggy air that gusted in from the alley. She took a step forward, stopped.

The front of the white enameled bureau was streaked with a reddish brown substance. Drops of it had spattered on the picture of her and her parents.

Her foot nudged something and she looked down. A knife—one from the kitchen rack—lay on the carpet, also crusted with red brown.

She bent to pick it up. Behind her Adam tensed. He said, "Don't touch it."

She straightened. Took it all in then. Her gaze moved around the room in a crazy hop-skip-jump pattern. Things registered, the way they do when a flashbulb explodes.

Big splash of red brown on the dirty beige couch, vivid at first, then fading to . . . jagged shards of glass on the carpet, curved glass, edges curled upward, glinting and . . . overnight bag tipped on its side, more of that stuff all over it and . . . feet in athletic shoes, the word *Nike* . . .

He lay on his stomach, blue-jeaned legs splayed, yellow sweater with more crusty brown.

Jesus, why is that stuff all over—

Adam pushed past her. She backed up against the wall. He knelt, blocking her view of the man on the floor, grabbing his wrist.

Joanna sucked in her breath, closed her eyes, fought for equilibrium. Opened them again and focused on the sofa bed . . .

Light blue jacket . . . down jacket . . . light blue down jacket with a rip in the pocket that he should have mended but

didn't and I only gave it to him last Christmas and now
he's...

"E.J.!"

Adam pivoted, face shocked and drained. He reached for
her, but she pushed him aside. Stared down into the face of
the dead man.

Not E.J.

Antony Parducci.

FIFTEEN

RELIEF CAME swiftly, followed by incredulity. Parducci—briefly her lover, long her enemy—dead? Here? *Dead in her own apartment?*

She twisted and looked at Adam, lips parted in a question she didn't know how to phrase.

He said, "Who is he?"

"Parducci."

Adam was silent, apparently at as much of a loss as she.

Joanna looked back at the dead man. His teeth were bared in a savage grimace; the electric blue of his deep-sunk eyes was dimmed; the scar on his neck from a long-ago thyroid operation stood out against his bloodless skin; one arm was stretched above his head, as if he'd been reaching for something when he died.

Her stomach spasmed and she began to shiver. She moved backward to get away from the body, bumping into Adam.

Adam said, "The police—"

"Yes."

"Where's the phone?"

"Isn't one. Go downstairs. Ask Rex."

He stood and hurried out without speaking.

Joanna straightened her clothing with excessive care. Went to stand in the hallway. Parducci's image accompanied her into the darkness there. When she closed her eyes it only became more vivid.

She kept thinking she should feel something besides shock and disbelief. Her youthful couplings with Parducci had been a disastrous mistake, undertaken without love or even affection, but the man *had* fathered her son. If she couldn't feel sorrow, why not regret, or at least pity? If none of those, why not satisfaction, vindication? After all, she'd spent a great many years hating him....

But she felt nothing that had to do with Parducci as a fellow human being—nothing to do with him as a man who had experienced fear and pain and death.

That, then, was what years of such hatred finally wrought: a lack of emotion, symptomatic of one's own brand of inhumanity.

After a few minutes footsteps sounded on the stairs. Adam returning.

"I called nine-eleven," he said. "Police'll be here soon."

She nodded.

"Joanna, what was Parducci doing here?"

"I don't know."

"How did he get in?"

She shrugged, incapable of further speech.

Adam's eyes narrowed. "He would have needed two keys to get in here; I saw you use that many. Is there something you're not telling... Joanna, what happened to E.J.?"

The sound of her son's name brought her out of herself—that, and the sirens in the distance. She pushed away from the wall and went back into the apartment. When Adam entered she was lifting E.J.'s jacket off the sofa bed. It too was speckled with Parducci's blood.

"Hey," Adam said, "don't touch anything."

She moved past him to the closet off the tiny foyer and took out a hanger. After putting the jacket on it, she pushed aside the row of old clothing that hung there and placed it at the very end, next to the wall. Then she rearranged the garments and shut the closet door.

Adam said, "Why did you do that?"

The sirens were very close now. She said, "It's E.J.'s. They can't know he was here. They'll think he killed Parducci."

"Why, for God's sake? That makes no sense—"

She went back to the hallway. There were voices at the foot of the stairway, one of them Rex's. The police had arrived. "Just don't say anything to them about E.J. Please. And try to get Rex aside and ask him not to mention it, either."

"Joanna, it's stupid to try to cover up. E.J. didn't even know Parducci—"

"He did! And when they find out—"

"You're talking nonsense."

"I'm not!" They were coming up the stairs now. She put her hand on Adam's arm, gripping it tightly. "Adam, listen to me: Parducci was...he was E.J.'s father."

He just looked at her, waiting.

"E.J. was adopted," she added.

Adam's eyes remained on her face, comprehension seeping into them. After a few seconds he said, "And you're his mother."

She merely nodded.

Adam took a deep breath, expelled it slowly. The police were on the second flight of stairs now.

She said, "Look, you don't even have to tell them you were inside my apartment. Just say you left me at the door and heard me scream when...that way you don't have to be involved in any of this."

"Why would I duck out on you now?"

"I'm thinking of your reputation. This could get messy. Most men in your position—"

"I'm not most men." He glanced past her at the far end of the hall and his posture straightened slightly. "It's okay, Joanna," he said in a louder voice. "The police are here now."

THE DETECTIVE in charge was named Gallagher; his round glasses made him look like an owl. He introduced his partner as Inspector Finch; in spite of the birdlike name, he resembled an overweight basset hound. They sent the

uniformed men who had arrived before them to see if any of
the neighbors were home, and asked preliminary questions
in the hallway. Then they had Joanna and Adam accompany them into the apartment and show them exactly what
they'd done and touched when they'd discovered the body.

After they'd finished, Gallagher pointed to the overnight
bag on the floor. "This yours, Mrs. Stark?"

"Yes."

"You just get home?"

"I don't live here. It's just a place I keep to stay in when
I'm in town."

"Where *do* you live?"

"Sonoma." She gave him her post office box number and
street address.

"So you just got into town."

"Last night."

"Would you go over your movements from the time you
arrived, please?"

Joanna glanced at Parducci's body. "Could we—?" She
motioned at the floor.

"Oh, sure. Lab crew's waiting to get in anyhow. Not
much room here."

They went outside; the corridor was crowded with people. Adam said, "Inspector Gallagher, maybe we could talk
downstairs in the bar? Mrs. Stark's had a bad shock, and
with all your people—"

"Sure, Mr. Hawthorne. Finch will take you down; he
needs to get started interviewing the people there."

Joanna felt a flash of alarm. "Why?" she asked. Adam's
fingers tightened warningly on her arm.

The inspector looked sharply at her. After a few beats he
said, "One of them may have seen something."

"I see. Sorry—I'm not tracking too well."

"Understandable, Mrs. Stark." Gallagher motioned for
Finch. "Take them downstairs, would you. They'll wait
while you check out the customers."

Adam propelled Joanna along, hand firmly on her elbow. As they started down the stairs he said, "What you need is a drink. I'll ask Rex if he has any decent brandy."

She nodded.

When they entered the bar, however, Finch motioned for them to sit in one of the side booths. "I'll check out that brandy for you," he said.

Rex stood in front of the bar, surrounded by curious, excited patrons. Finch moved toward him, and Joanna cast a panicky glance at Adam.

"Sorry," he said. "I tried."

"It's not your fault. Maybe Rex won't think to mention seeing E.J."

The New Apia was the liveliest she'd ever seen it. Customers milled around, all talking at once. An old man in a pin-striped suit and a bowler with a small red feather was expounding in the loud tones of one who is somewhat deaf. "It's what you get for renting to an outsider, Rex," he said. "She's never there, she doesn't care about the place, and now look what's happened."

It surprised her, because she hadn't thought any of the bar patrons were aware of her existence, or that they considered her an outsider. Now she realized there was some truth in what the man had said: She'd become a stranger to the neighborhood and its people.

Finch shouldered through the crowd around Rex and spoke briefly with him. Rex went behind the bar and returned with a bottle and two glasses. Finch brought them to the booth and departed.

Joanna said, "Why isn't he letting us talk to anybody? Does he think one of us killed Parducci?"

"At this stage, they probably suspect everybody." But Adam's eyes were worried. He opened the brandy bottle and poured some into the glasses.

Joanna toyed with her snifter, unwilling to cloud her mental processes with more alcohol. Minutes went by—ten, fifteen, twenty. Finch spoke at length with Rex, then left the bar for a while. When he came back he made the round of the customers. Adam seemed lost in thought; Joanna supposed he was regretting his refusal to "duck out" on her. The bar clock showed eleven-ten when Gallagher finally came through the door.

He conferred with Finch for a few minutes. Then both men approached the booth where Joanna and Adam sat. Gallagher said, "Mr. Hawthorne, Inspector Finch needs to ask you some questions. Maybe you could move to that empty booth." He indicated one near the far end of the room.

Adam looked at Joanna, shrugged, and followed Finch. Gallagher sat opposite her.

"Okay, Mrs. Stark," he said, "let's talk about what you've been doing since you arrived in town."

She took a deep breath and related what had happened since she'd arrived at the New Apia more than twenty-four hours earlier. Gallagher took notes, reacting only once— when she mentioned having spent many of those hours in the company of Lieutenant John Brady. When she finished, he took off his glasses and polished them on a cocktail napkin before speaking.

"Well," he said, "it appears you were with a member of the Department at the time of the killing. We'll have to verify all this, of course."

"Of course. When *was* Mr. Parducci killed?"

"Medical examiner places it between midnight and eight this morning. That's an estimate, but given the degree of rigor—but you don't want me to go into that."

She nodded distractedly. E.J. had arrived after Rex closed up, sometime after two. "How was he killed?"

"Stab wound in the chest. Severed an artery, which accounts for the blood spattering."

She shuddered and gripped the brandy snifter harder, then drank some, swallowing convulsively. The cheap liquor tasted awful, burned going down. She pushed the glass away.

Gallagher was watching her closely. It occurred to her that he had volunteered the grisly details in order to throw her off balance. She took her hands off the table, lacing her fingers together where he couldn't see them, and said, "I see."

He let the silence lengthen. After a moment he asked, "What was your relationship with Mr. Parducci?"

"Relationship? I wouldn't call it that. He was a broker—a man who arranges art thefts. I own a security firm—Security Systems International—that specializes in protecting artworks."

"So your connection to him was professional?"

"Yes."

"In what way?"

"I'm sorry?"

"Was he an informant, or—"

"Oh, nothing like that. Parducci is . . . apprehending him was something of a crusade of mine. I've been responsible for thwarting a couple of his attempted thefts."

"Including this one at Renfrow's, or in addition to that?"

"In addition." She explained in greater detail.

Gallagher took more notes, then studied the pad, toying with his pen. "Why do you think Mr. Parducci was in your apartment?"

"I suppose he planned to harm me. He must have held a grudge."

"And how do you think he got in there?"

"I don't know. The window was open when Mr. Hawthorne and I found him, but I know I locked it before I left last night."

"There was no sign of forced entry on it—or on the door."

She was silent, thinking of her Sonoma house: It had shown no signs of forced entry, either. And then she thought of E.J.'s key ring, which had temporarily disappeared the day Parducci had taken *Dark Star*: It also contained keys to the apartment.

"Could Mr. Parducci have obtained a key somehow?" Gallagher asked.

"I don't see how."

"Does anyone besides you have a key?"

". . . No."

"Not even your stepson?"

Her fingers clenched. She fought to maintain her calm facade. "My stepson?"

"The bartender says your stepson, E.J.—what does that stand for?"

"Elliot. Elliot John Stark."

Gallagher noted it on his pad. "The bartender says he saw him entering the street door to the apartments at around two-twenty this morning."

She pretended to think. "That's possible. E.J. *does* have a set of keys, in case he wants to use the place."

"Did you know he intended to use it last night?"

"No."

"Did you see any sign that he'd been there when you returned and found Mr. Parducci's body?"

"No."

"Did you look in the closet?"

"The—?"

Now Gallagher leaned across the table toward her, his voice harsher. "The closet, Mrs. Stark."

"Why would I—"

"There's a man's jacket in the closet. Light blue, down, with a rip in one pocket. Does that sound familiar to you?"

"I'm . . . not sure."

"Does your stepson own a jacket like that?"

"I . . . maybe."

"Maybe? I understand from Mr. Malauulu that your stepson lives with you. Are you telling me you don't know what kind of jacket he wears?"

"He's a grown man, Inspector. I don't keep an inventory of his wardrobe. Besides, that jacket could belong to anyone who had visited me—"

"The jacket is covered with a blood-spatter pattern similar to that on the sofa. And there is a place on the sofa about the size of the jacket that contains no spatters."

She lowered her eyes and stared down at her clasped hands.

After a moment Gallagher spoke more gently. "Mrs. Stark, is there anything you can tell me that might explain your stepson's visit to your apartment?"

"No. I assume he intended to sleep there, rather than drive home."

"Is he a violent man? Would he attack if he thought he had surprised a burglar, for instance?"

Gallagher was offering her a possible excuse for E.J. having killed Parducci—but it was also a trap. She told the truth. "E.J. is the world's original pacifist. I've never seen him raise a hand to anyone."

"What if *he* were attacked?"

"I . . . don't know."

"Is E.J. aware of your efforts to entrap Mr. Parducci?"

"Yes."

"What does he think about them?"

"He thinks I'm obsessed, and wishes I would let go of it. So does my business partner. People are always saying I'm obsessed. I guess I present a pretty pathetic figure." She was surprised at the degree of bitterness in her own words.

And at Gallagher's reaction. He said mildly, "People with a mission always seem foolish to those who don't have one." Then he looked down at his pad, underlined a couple of things, snapped it closed, and stood.

"We've requested the Sonoma authorities to pick up your stepson and hold him for questioning," he added. "It would be best if you didn't try to contact him beforehand. Concocting alibis or excuses only makes things worse. And the

situation may not be as bad as it seems on the surface. There
was a gun under the body—Saturday night special. That
makes it look as if it could have been self-defense."

A gun...

Joanna stared at Gallagher, not really seeing him. The
presence of the gun unnerved her, made her aware of the
trap she had nearly walked into. Parducci had banked on her
realizing he was after the much-publicized Van Gogh and
that she would come to the city to try to prevent the theft.
He'd somehow gotten hold of E.J.'s keys to the apartment
and copied them. He'd known she would eventually show
up there, so he'd let himself in and waited. Waited to kill
her.

Joanna swallowed hard. Parducci's plan had very nearly
worked. If she hadn't left for the auction house when she
had last night...or if she'd returned before he'd been
killed...or if his timing had been slightly different in any of
a dozen ways...

Hours after killing her he would have collected the Van
Gogh and been on the next plane to wherever his client re-
sided, safe. Their perilously balanced game of cat and
mouse would have ended forever, with Parducci the victor.
And Joanna would have lost far more than just one final
round.

Gallagher was watching her. After a moment he said, "I'd
like a formal statement from you, Mrs. Stark. Say, eleven
tomorrow morning?"

She nodded. "Is it all right if I go home to Sonoma? Obviously I can't spend the night there." She motioned at the
ceiling.

"I have no problem with that. But remember what I
said—if you see your stepson, try to impress upon him that
it's in his best interests to cooperate with us." Gallagher
moved toward the door of the bar. Joanna saw Finch rise
from the rear booth and follow him.

Adam was coming toward her now, his face furrowed by lines of concern. When he reached the table he said something, but she missed the words entirely. She was hearing other words, uttered two days before: E.J. speaking of Parducci when she'd told him she thought he meant to kill her.

Just let him try. Let the bastard try, and I'll kill him first.

SIXTEEN

THERE WERE THREE vehicles in the dark parking area at the winery—the company truck, Joe Donatello's pickup, and a light-colored Jaguar sedan. No sign of E.J.'s motorcycle, no sheriff's car.

Joanna pulled her Fiat close to the crumbling retaining wall, got out, and ran toward the big double doors of the tasting room. Its windows were black behind the climbing ivy. She pounded on the doors anyway, but got no response. After a moment she set off through the thick shrubbery toward the rear wing, where both the lab and the space E.J. and Joe intended to use as living quarters were located.

It was close to one-thirty in the morning. After the police had left the New Apia she'd had some difficulty getting free of Rex and Adam. Rex was suffering pangs of guilt for having told about seeing E.J. He'd kept berating himself for his stupidity, and wanted to make amends by putting Joanna up at a vacant apartment in another building he owned. She'd had no success convincing him she would be better off at home until Loni—whose rare appearance downstairs had been prompted by the evening's commotion—reminded her husband that the police had held Joanna's blood-spattered suitcase as evidence. A girl, Loni said, couldn't do without her makeup and nightie.

Adam was an entirely different problem. He'd heard her in the phone booth, unsuccessfully calling around for E.J. And he'd been determined to go with Joanna and help her find her son before the police did. She was in no shape to drive, he said; she'd had no sleep the night before. When she pointed out that he hadn't slept either, he shrugged it off. When she said she didn't want to involve him in violating a police order, he said he was already involved. In the end she'd had to be very firm with him, and he'd gone off looking put out and threatening to raise hell if she didn't appear at the Hall of Justice for her statement the next morning.

On the way home, however, she began to wish she had let him accompany her. The drive north seemed to take much longer than usual; her muscles pulled rigid with tension, and her eyes kept jerking to the rearview mirror, searching for imaginary pursuers. The image of Parducci's body kept flashing before her: Parducci, the brief passion of her youth; Parducci, the nemesis of the intervening years. She'd tracked him relentlessly, twice come close to trapping him, and now his death had cheated her of the final triumph. She was surprised to find she felt a fresh rage toward him—because he had eluded that final, long-awaited confrontation.

And with the rage came a consuming curiosity: Who had killed the man she'd considered her own personal quarry? Worried as she was about E.J., the gut-level instincts she always relied on, coupled with the less dependable faith of a mother in her child, told her there was an explanation for what seemed to be evidence against him.

Who *was* the guilty party, then? Someone who hadn't wanted the theft of the Van Gogh to come off. Someone who knew of her connection to Parducci. Someone who had lured him to the apartment. Perhaps someone who wanted to place the blame for his death on her.

No, that didn't make sense. Parducci must have had keys to both the Sonoma house and the apartment. He'd gone there of his own volition.

Someone who had followed him to the apartment, then? Or someone he himself had summoned there? No, *that* didn't make sense, either. If he'd gone there to settle his score with her, he would not have wanted a witness....

When she finally reached Sonoma, she stopped at the phone booth outside the Shell station on Broadway and called Sally Jane, the one person she knew who would be able to find out if E.J. had already been taken into custody, but reached only her machine. A quick check of Old Winery Road revealed a police car stationed across from her own driveway. After that she headed up the valley. E.J.'s ownership of the winery, she reasoned, was not yet common knowledge. The sheriff's department—it was in county jurisdiction—might not have checked there.

Now as she skirted the old stone building, the night seemed very dark. One of the winds that frequently whipped through the valley had kicked up; it rattled the leaves of the ivy and made her light jacket billow. She shivered and pulled it closer, ducking under some low-hanging branches and stepping out of the shrubbery.

Ahead of her was a concrete pad on which the stainless steel dejuicers, presses, and tanks stood. A floodlight near the roofline of the rear wing made the elephantlike snout of one of the cone-shaped dejuicers gleam in all its gaudy newness. Joanna made her way through the five tall tanks and approached the doorway behind them. The windows that flanked it were opaque rectangles of light. She knocked and waited impatiently.

After a moment a chain rattled and the door opened. She looked in at Joe Donatello.

"Joanna—are you okay?" he said.

She pushed through the door, stumbling slightly. "Is he here—" she began, then stopped abruptly.

The room was in chaos, unpacked crates and boxes piled everywhere, but in its center was a small oasis of order containing a card table and three chairs. Two of them were currently occupied. As Joanna glanced questioningly at Joe, Robert Donatello rose to greet her. Of course, she thought, the Jaguar in the parking area.

"Mrs. Stark." Donatello bowed in a formal old-world way.

Joanna didn't reply; she was looking at the woman who remained seated. Veronica Donatello was easily recognizable from her campaign photos: strongly built, with a sleek cap of black hair and a hawklike nose. Even at this late hour she was made up as if for a television appearance, her full lips a carmine that matched her long lacquered nails. She did not smile as her hard eyes regarded Joanna.

Joanna felt an instant visceral dislike of the woman, followed quickly by annoyance. What were these people doing here? She needed to talk with Joe in private.

Donatello came forward, put a hand on her arm, and steered her to the empty chair. "Mrs. Stark," he said, "we heard about your son's trouble, and we came right over." He paused, then added, "Allow me to introduce my granddaughter, Veronica."

Veronica barely acknowledged the introduction. She continued to stare at Joanna—appraisingly, as if she were trying to decide the best way to win her vote. Joanna nodded abruptly and looked back at Joe. He stood near the door, his posture so rigid that she could almost feel his tension. To his grandfather she said, "How did you hear? There wasn't enough time for the news to have made even the late broadcasts."

"I like to listen to the police band at night. When I heard the call to pick up your son, I was naturally concerned, so I phoned a man I know at the SFPD."

"You were 'naturally concerned'? Why?"

He made a smoothing motion with his hands, as if to quell her rising anger. "Your son is my grandson's business partner—"

"Your grandson is my son's *employee*."

Donatello shrugged and sat down without replying.

Joe stepped forward. "Joanna, you look tired. Can I give you a drink? Some coffee?"

It was an obvious attempt to normalize the situation, but the unsteadiness in his voice rendered it ineffectual. Joanna tried to control her own agitation, and said, "Coffee will be fine, thank you," and watched him hurry through the door that led to the living quarters.

When she turned back to his sister and grandfather, they were looking at each other, a silent current of communication passing between them. "So," she said, "you checked with the SFPD and then rushed right over here."

"Joey needed to know," Veronica said.

"Couldn't you have just phoned?"

"We thought it best to talk with him in person."

"Why?"

Veronica started to speak, but her grandfather tapped his fingers on the table to silence her. She looked away, mouth tightening irritably. He said, "I wanted to impress upon him what a scandal could do to this ill-advised venture he has entered into. It could destroy it, to say nothing of his good name. Perhaps now he'll come back where he belongs—"

"Joe has a two-year contract with Stark Vineyards. He's also a grown man, capable of making his own decisions. He doesn't appear to be pleased with your meddling."

The old man's eyes flashed, but he merely said, "What concerns one Donatello concerns all."

Joe returned to the room, a coffee mug in hand. "What Grandfather means," he said in a voice made rough by anger of his own, "is that he's concerned for *his* good name— and Ronnie's. He came here to find out if I had personal knowledge of the murder. He's afraid that my connection with E.J. might have an adverse affect on her campaign."

Veronica glanced up at her brother, her carmine lips contemptuous. "It's a legitimate concern, Joey."

Joe's hand shook as he gave the mug to Joanna. "Your concern, not mine."

"One would think you didn't want your sister to succeed," Robert Donatello said.

"I don't care whether she does or not. I told you the other day, I'm through with this family. I've done the last—"

"You can never be through with your family." Donatello rose, signaling for Veronica to do likewise. "We'll leave now. Your attitude makes this conversation counterproductive." He nodded to Joanna. "Mrs. Stark."

Veronica stood, fixed Joe with a final scornful glance, and trailed out after her grandfather.

Joe watched them leave, arms stiff at his sides. When the door closed, he whirled and slammed his fist down on one of the packing cases. "Damn them and their arrogance!"

Joanna wasn't interested in his family conflict. She said, "Joe, have you heard from E.J.?"

He brought himself under control, not without effort. "The last time was around seven yesterday evening. We'd planned to go to Ronnie's benefit wine auction with Karla Perelli; she wanted to show us how some of her clients were using an event like that for promotional purposes. But E.J. begged off. He said he had a late dinner date in the city."

"With whom?"

"He didn't give a name. But he said it was someone who would advise him on what to do about his father."

"You know Parducci was his father?"

"Of course. I've known for a long time." At Joanna's surprised look, he added, "E.J.'s my best friend. Friends share things like that."

She was about to retort that he didn't need to instruct her in the art of friendship, but she held her tongue. After all, she was no expert on the subject. The habit of withholding the vulnerable core of herself was too strongly ingrained for true friendship with anyone. Not even David had fully broken through that reserve. It was a personal failing that, when she thought about it, saddened and discouraged her.

"Joanna?" Joe said. "Don't be angry with E.J. for telling me."

"Why would I be? He has a right to confide in anyone he chooses. Did he come here Thursday night after we quarreled?"

Joe nodded. "He felt terrible about it. He has a lot of guilt where you're concerned."

"Why?"

"Because he knows how much you sacrificed for him. And he remembers all the ways he hurt you before he knew you were his mother."

Yet another hidden side to her son. E.J. was right: She did underrate him. "Joe, where do you think he is now?"

"I've no idea, but I wouldn't worry. If he can prove he didn't kill Parducci, he'll go to the cops and tell them. If not, he'll stay away from the places they'll look for him."

She hesitated, then asked a question that for her was rhetorical, intended to find out if Joe shared her faith in E.J. "Do you think he did kill him?"

Joe's reply was immediate. "For God's sake, no! There's no way E.J. could kill anyone."

AS SHE LAY in bed in the dark hours of the morning, the wind rattled the glass in its frames and set the surrounding shrubbery to scraping against the exterior walls. The police car had still been stationed on the road when she'd returned; she knew if she looked outside it would be there now. She listened for the sound of E.J.'s motorcycle, hoped to hear it, yet hoped not to. And she thought of her son, out there in the wind-tossed darkness.

He must be badly frightened. Now that she'd had time to think it through, she could guess what had happened: E.J. had gone to the apartment between the time she'd left and when Parducci arrived. He'd changed from his traveling clothes—hence the jacket on the couch—and kept his dinner date. When he'd come back, he'd found his father's body. But where he'd gone and what he'd done after that she couldn't imagine. She only knew he was afraid, and she longed to comfort him.

Such a difference, she thought, from her feelings at their last parting. The resentment toward him no longer simmered inside her. She could remember it, identify clear instances of it through all the years, but it no longer lived. Why? What had changed?

Well, for one thing, she'd begun making concrete plans to get on with her life—such as giving up the apartment, involving herself fully in the business. Since E.J.'s birth she'd consistently passed up opportunities, allowed his existence to dictate the terms of her own. But it was *she* who had allowed that. And, she thought, what after all is resentment but misdirected anger at oneself? Once that anger is recognized for what it is, resentment cannot thrive.

But the larger component in the change was Parducci's death. It removed all threat of harm to her and E.J.; it relieved her of her self-imposed need to protect her son. For the first time in twenty-three years, she realized, she was truly free. And with that realization, in spite of her concern for E.J., sleep finally came.

AT EIGHT in the morning, Joanna sat down to a task she dreaded. She had to brace herself for a full ten minutes before she consulted her Rolodex and called the unfamiliar number in Tenafly, New Jersey. As the phone began to ring, she thought, Please don't let her answer....

Her plea was denied. A pleasant, low-timbred female voice said, "Scherer residence."

For a few seconds Joanna couldn't speak. Then she said, "Millie?"

"Yes?"

"It's...Joanna." She'd been about to give her whole name, but that was ridiculous. Her father's second wife knew perfectly well who she was, even if they'd never spoken.

There was a pause. "Well. Joanna." The woman's voice was surprised, but then a cautious note of warmth crept into it. "Joanna, how are you?"

"Not very good. Is my father there?"

"I'm sorry, it's one of his days at the clinic. Is there anything I can do?"

She barely heard the question. "The clinic? He's not ill?"

Millie replied with a touch of amusement, "No, the *legal* clinic. It's a service run by retired lawyers, for low-income families. Your father puts in a couple of days a week."

"Oh. I didn't know."

"Of course you couldn't." There was no reproach in the statement. "Now tell me what's wrong, and I'll get in touch with him."

Strangely it seemed quite natural to unburden herself to this woman she'd once sworn never to speak to. "I know that E.J. came there once before, when he found out about Parducci," she concluded, "and I thought he might this time."

"We haven't heard from him, but that doesn't mean he won't just show up. If he does, where can we reach you?"

Joanna began to bristle at Millie's use of "we." After all, this was a family matter. Then she thought, They've been married for nearly twenty-five years, for God's sake! What is she, if not family?

"Joanna?" Now Millie seemed worried.

Quickly she gave the number at SSI, then added Adam's office number as well. He'd said he would meet her at the Hall of Justice, and she assumed she would have as much difficulty getting free of him then as she had the previous night. Besides, she wasn't really sure she *wanted* to be free of him.

"Do you want your father to call you back?" Millie asked. "Or shall I tell him to wait until he hears from one or the other of you?"

She'd spoken with him fewer than half a dozen times since she'd left home, all of them in the past year or so, and she wasn't sure she could deal with another conversation with a closely related stranger. She said, "Not unless he hears from E.J." Then, remembering he had a heart condition, she added, "Try not to upset him. It'll probably turn out just fine."

"I always try to take good care of him."

"I'm sure you do."

There was an awkward silence, but then Millie said, "Your father's awfully fond of E.J. It meant a great deal to him to get to know his grandson. It would mean even more to him to get reacquainted with you. To me, also."

It was disconcerting, Joanna realized, to finally confront a person you'd set up as a villain and find she wasn't one at all. For a moment she remained silent, unable to let go of a grudge nearly a quarter of a century old. Then she smiled wryly, picturing herself as a grown-up child who doesn't quite want to leave off pouting yet. "Thank you, Millie," she said. "Maybe after all this is cleared up, E.J. and I will visit."

The relief in her stepmother's voice as they ended their conversation matched that which was spreading through Joanna.

ADAM WASN'T AT SAN FRANCISCO'S Hall of Justice when she arrived at eleven, and for the next two hours she barely had time to think of him. The formal statement turned out to be much more than a formality; E.J.'s prolonged unavailability had elevated him to prime-suspect status, and Inspector Gallagher questioned her in far greater detail about her son and his presumed relationship with Antony Parducci. She adamantly denied there was any relationship at all, gave minimal answers to most of his questions, and was on the verge of requesting that she be allowed to consult with her attorney when Gallagher received an urgent phone call and abruptly ended the session.

Joanna left the monolithic gray building hurriedly, wondering if the call had concerned E.J. It was possible he'd been apprehended or come forward with an explanation. But if so, the fact that Gallagher hadn't chosen to tell her made the picture bleak....

Halfway to the garage where she'd left her car she paused, realizing she'd forgotten to look around the Hall for Adam. It was odd she hadn't run into him: He was scheduled to give a statement at the same time and had been very definite about meeting her. Since SSI's building wasn't all that far away, she decided to leave her car where it was, walk over there, and call him.

When she arrived an unfamiliar security man was in the lobby; the offices held a Sunday afternoon hush. A stranger at the best of times, she now felt like an interloper. When she called Renfrow's, she was once again informed that Mr. Hawthorne was in conference and couldn't be disturbed. With a sense of déjà vu, she left SSI's number. Next she tried calling Nick, on the off chance that E.J. might have contacted him, but the message on his machine said he and his lady would be out of town until Tuesday. Finally she flipped through her Rolodex and began making calls to old friends, acquaintances, business associates—anyone with whom E.J. might conceivably have consulted about Parducci over dinner on Friday.

The calls elicited nothing except amazement from a number of people whom she hadn't contacted in years. A few had heard about Parducci's murder on the newscasts and were eager to discuss it, but she brushed their questions aside and terminated the conversations. When she finished it was after four o'clock. A final call to Renfrow's proved Adam still to be in conference—odd for a Sunday after an important sale had been wrapped up. She decided to drive over there.

Bill, the elderly security guard, had come on duty. As usual he sat transfixed by his small portable TV. Joanna was signing out when she heard the words, "Enormous art fraud."

Quickly she moved behind the guard, where she could see the screen.

The news commentator was saying, "The painting, *Flowers along the Rhone*, was sold yesterday afternoon by Renfrow's Auctioneers for a staggering sixty-eight million dollars. But now the successful bidder, an unidentified Tokyo insurance firm, claims it has been contacted by an expert who can prove that the Van Gogh, along with a sister painting, were stolen in France shortly after the First World War. Although the statute of limitations on the theft has run out, title to this work and its sister, *The Vineyard at Marmande*, is in dispute, and a civil suit may be filed . . ."

The Vineyard at Marmande! Joanna's breath caught and she stared transfixed at the TV. All the time she'd been thinking it was an actual vineyard, when it was really a painting—yet another stolen Van Gogh. And apparently it had literally been under her nose—in the possession of her "almost relative," Davis Deane!

SEVENTEEN

"THE WORST PART is that this whole thing could have been prevented if I'd only been willing to *listen* to the guy." Adam slumped in the rear booth at the New Apia, his face haggard. He pulled at the knot of his tie, then took a swallow of scotch.

In retrospect it seemed strange to Joanna that they'd come to Rex's bar to talk, but at the time it had presented one of the few handy refuges from the army of reporters who had clustered outside Renfrow's, insisting on the public's (largely overrated) right to know. Now she felt more than a little oppressed; she kept trying to push aside the thought of the apartment upstairs and what had happened there. Only a few patrons were seated at the bar. Rex was wiping off the tables, covertly glancing their way from time to time. Their unexplained agitation seemed to have infected him; his movements were oddly erratic and jumpy.

She said, "Tell me again—what's the man's name?"

"Eschler. Claude Eschler. Art historian from Geneva, Switzerland. Man with a passion." Adam raised his glass, smiling bitterly. "Here's to men with passions."

"An old man?"

"In his early eighties. Maybe if he'd been younger our appraisers would have taken him more seriously. Maybe I'd have agreed to talk with him—but I don't know. You see, I wanted to make the big splash on Saturday. We all did."

"He has personal knowledge of the theft of the paintings?"

"Next best thing—he interviewed several individuals who did. The guy's an armchair art detective; he studies unsolved cases. The theft of *Flowers* and that other one has intrigued him for years. When the news of my auction hit the papers and Eschler saw the photos of the painting, he recognized it as one nobody had laid eyes on since it was stolen in Paris in nineteen-nineteen. He got excited, took the first flight here armed with all kinds of documentation. Came straight to Renfrow's—and got the brushoff. So he got mad, and after the auction he followed Tokaido's rep to her hotel and laid out the whole thing for her.''

''And rather than come to you for clarification, she held a press conference.''

''Yeah—the bitch.''

Joanna was silent. Although it was a surprising turn of events, she wasn't sure the revelation about *Flowers along the Rhone* had anything to do with Parducci's plan to steal the painting or his murder. Had it not been for Davis Deane's apparent connection with the sister painting, *The Vineyard at Marmande* . . .

The painting had to be in Deane's possession, probably hidden somewhere at the resort. But where? And how had Deane acquired it in the first place? He would have been only nineteen at the time it was stolen, but a great many young Americans had been in Paris at the end of the First World War. Was Deane one of those?

Too many questions, she thought. And until she had answers, she wasn't willing to discuss the sister painting with Adam. He had enough on his mind. Besides, her feeling of kinship with Deane prompted her to protect the old man, at least until she knew what his part in the confused history of the two Van Goghs really was.

''So what happens now?'' she asked.

''Eschler's story will have to be checked out. I need to contact Jerry Eckridge and make him tell me where he got the painting. Unfortunately he's nowhere to be found.''

''Do you suppose he knows what's happened?''

"If he watches the TV news, he does. The folks in my office'll keep trying to reach him, both here in the city and at his Glen Ellen place, but in the meantime the press is having a fine time, and Renfrow's reputation is washing down the sewer."

"What will happen to the painting?"

Adam shrugged. "The family that originally owned it are all dead, and even if they weren't, Jerry's title to it is legal after all these years. But as to whether Tokaido will still want it—who knows?"

"And if they don't, Renfrow's is out six point eight million in commission."

"That's about it."

She studied him, surprised at what struck her as really a very mild reaction. While he appeared weary and self-reproachful, she saw no evidence of rage or self-pity. "How come you're not tearing your hair and screaming?"

He tipped his half-empty glass and crunched on an ice cube. "Wouldn't do any good. Remember what I said last night about the auction maybe having been my moment? Well, I guess it wasn't. So that means there's another somewhere down the pike." He smiled ruefully, then changed the subject. "Any sign of your son?"

"No. While I was waiting for you at Renfrow's I checked with my reporter friend. The sheriff's department located his motorcycle in a park-and-ride lot outside of Sonoma, but he hasn't been picked up yet."

"It's just as well, until the murder is cleared up."

"You believe he's innocent, and you don't even know him."

"I can't believe that a man who was raised by David Stark and who is your own son would kill anyone."

"That's the way I feel, expect when I think of Parducci. He has his blood, too. Parducci was insane toward the end. He killed a couple of people that I know of. I saw his victims, in London and in Cornwall—"

"You're not beginning to doubt E.J.'s innocence?"

"Not really. But I wonder about heredity."

"Heredity, environment—the psychologists are always squabbling over that one. You know what I think? None of it matters worth a damn. We are what we are. E.J. is what he is. And according to what you tell me, what he is *isn't* a killer."

It was exactly the kind of reassurance she'd been seeking. She smiled gratefully at him.

He added, "I was hoping that tonight you'd tell me about you and Parducci, but I can see now's not the time."

"No, it's not." She touched the back of his hand lightly. "Thanks for understanding."

"If there's anything I can do to help—"

"I know."

They were both silent for a while. Joanna sensed that Adam—in spite of his encouraging words to her and his philosophical stance about the Van Gogh disaster—was as deeply mired in his own bog of depression as she was in hers.

She had reached that bleak moment that every parent faces at least once—when he or she realizes that no amount of love or effort or wishful thinking is going to miraculously make everything right again. Tears came to her eyes and she thought angrily, Why did our parents lie to us? Why were we raised to think the world wasn't so goddamned unfair and dangerous? And why did we lie to our own kids? Wouldn't it be easier for all of us to live with the truth, so that when our lives get screwed up by random circumstances, we wouldn't be so shocked and helpless?

Up until this moment she'd considered herself a cynic, nurtured on years of painfully gleaned experience. Now she realized that on some level she still must believe the force-fed fairy tale. Worse yet, wanted to believe it.

Okay, she told herself, if you believe it, do something to make it come true. Try to protect your son this one last time.

She brushed her tears away and said to Adam, "Maybe we can help each other."

WHEN SHE ARRIVED at Sonoma Valley Hospital at a little after eight, she was told Davis Deane was still in critical condition and was allowed no visitors. For a moment she thought about going to see Karla Perelli, but decided that Deane's great-granddaughter—given the fact that she'd been estranged from the old man until recently—would be unable to answer her questions. For them, she needed to talk with Deane himself. In the end she set out for Glen Ellen to attempt to track down Jerry Eckridge, a task she had undertaken both for herself and Adam.

She drove toward the plaza, intending to take Highway 12 through town and up the valley to the Glen Ellen turn-off, but found traffic blocked. The center of Sonoma was clogged with cars and people; red and blue banners and bunting decked a platform in front of city hall. Joanna vaguely recalled something about a Donatello rally being scheduled for that evening—one of the last all-out efforts before Tuesday's election. She made a U-turn and cut over to Arnold Drive, bypassing town, and followed the two-lane highway up the tunnel of trees on the spacious grounds of Sonoma State Hospital and past the cluster of buildings—country store, Jack London Lodge, cafés, real estate offices—that comprised the village of Glen Ellen. Beyond it she took the turnoff for Morton's Hot Springs, consulted Adam's hastily scrawled directions, and began watching for Sonoma Mountain Road. It appeared on her left, narrowed almost immediately, and began to climb in gentle switch-backs.

The sun had sunk behind the mountains, but its afterglow spilled over them, filtering through the shadows and staining them pinkish gray. Trees—oak, buckeye, eucalyptus, fir—stood out in black relief; the hollows of the hills and rock-strewn gullies where a small stream ran were deeply purpled. Occasionally a house stood close to the road; more often there would be gates guarding the winding driveways of ranches and country estates. The land was wild and overgrown in places; fenced for horse pasture in others; frequently covered with vineyards. In the ten minutes she drove along the winding road, she didn't encounter a single car.

When her odometer indicated she'd come three miles it was dusk and she had to turn on her headlights. She began scanning the right-hand roadside for the gate to the Eckridge property. Adam—who had been there a number of times back in the days when Jerry and Sandra threw lavish Fourth of July barbecues—had described it as an odd sculpted metal arch, "sort of like if you'd bent two drill bits and stuck them in the ground so they came together." When she spied them, she had to admit the effect was startling— and not particularly aesthetic.

The blacktop drive that snaked away beyond the gates was in better shape than the potholed road she'd just traveled over. It climbed a hill, flanked on either side by vineyards. When she reached the top of the rise, she saw a sprawling shingle and glass house, several outbuildings, a tennis court and swimming pool—all snuggled down into a dell among more vineyards. The darkness had deepened now, with the suddenness of mountain country, and she couldn't tell the make of the car parked in the semicircular area in front of the house, nor that of the one coming away from there, its headlights glaring on high beam.

The drive was not wide enough for two vehicles. The other car seemed to be moving fast. Joanna glanced to either side, saw there was a deep drainage ditch between the blacktop and the vineyard. She flicked the Fiat's lights to warn the other car.

It kept coming.

Alarmed, she flicked the lights again, leaned on the horn. Its polite European beep seemed weak and ineffectual.

The other car seemed to speed up. Its headlights blurred the travel smears and dirt on the Fiat's windshield. Joanna had a brief impression of pale gray and fairly good size, but that was all.

Frantically she twisted the steering wheel to her right. As the car skidded off the blacktop the wheel wrenched free of her hands. There was a shearing of metal, a violent impact that flung her sideways across the transmission hump. And then an even more jarring crash...

EIGHTEEN

SHOCK BLURRED her perceptions. She lay with her eyes shut, her head jammed against something, something else binding tightly across her breasts. Tires squealed down the driveway. When the noise faded, she heard nothing but her own labored breathing.

She opened her eyes and saw the door of the glovebox, sprung open by the crash. Her right arm was pinned under her, against the passenger seat. She raised the left one, felt above her head, found she was wedged against the door handle. The car canted to that side, enough for the seatbelt to pull painfully. She wiggled around, reached its fastening, unhooked it.

Slowly she sat up, wincing as the gearshift dug into her hip. The drainage ditch rose five feet or so on either side of the car, its weedy vegetation illuminated by the headlights. The Fiat rested lopsidedly at the bottom of the depression.

Her equilibrium gradually returned. The Fiat had stalled; she reached for the keys and turned the ignition off, thinking of electrical sparks, gas leaks, explosions. Then she made a careful physical inventory: top of head, tender; neck, some pain; arms okay; legs okay; pain across chest where the seatbelt had bound, diminishing. No other evidence of injury, but that didn't mean it wouldn't surface later. As for the car—she couldn't begin to assess the damage. All she knew was that it wouldn't emerge from this ditch without the aid of a tow truck.

And what about the son of a bitch who had run her off the driveway? Why hadn't he stopped? What kind of person just keeps coming at you, runs you into a ditch, and then takes off? Someone like the driver of the truck that had forced Davis Deane off the highway...

"Oh," she said. Sat very still and thought about that for a moment. Then she fumbled around on the floor until she found her purse. Crawled out of the car and climbed the steep embankment.

The Eckridge house lay about a quarter-mile away at the bottom of the hill. The car she'd seen earlier still stood in its parking area. Despite the commotion of the crash, no one had appeared. She hesitated, realized there was no place else within easy walking distance, and set off that way.

The night was full dark now, with only a luminescent purple shaping the tops of the western hills. The house and outbuildings were featureless rectangles, their edges blurring into the blackness. A bird cried once, shrilly. Joanna's skin prickled, and she wrapped her arms around herself. The motion caused a stab of pain across her right shoulder and down her arm.

She neared the house, guided by a faint glow behind a front-facing window. The window was large; its triangular upper portion extended toward the cathedral-style peak of the roof. The light, muted by what appeared to be mini-blinds, revealed nothing more than overgrown shrubbery close to the wall. Joanna reached into her purse and located her flashlight, shone it on the car that stood several yards away. It was a luxury sedan, one of those American makes that she could never identify from its brethren; its personalized license plate read JME 1—Jerry Eckridge's.

She turned toward the house and trained her flash downward on the flagstone path. The shrubs next to the front door were also high; she brushed at them and found a bell push under the branches. The chimes played four bars of a tune she couldn't quite place.

No answer. She rang twice again, then went back down the path, looking from the dark sedan to the glowing window. The lights might have been left on for security; Jerry could have gone out in another vehicle. He might even have been the driver of the car that had run her into the ditch....

Whatever the situation here, she needed to get to a phone. After a moment's indecision, she started around the house toward the outbuildings, thinking someone might be in one of them. When she reached the rear she saw light spilling through a wall of glass overlooking the swimming pool. Inside was a casual living room: fireplace flanked by a pair of big L-shaped couches, pool table, wet bar. Joanna skirted the pool and Jacuzzi and went up to the sliding door.

Track lighting shone down on the bar. Chrome floor lamps of a curving stemmed style popular two or three years ago hung over the couches. On a low table between them sat a partially eaten pizza still in its box and a half-full mug of beer. The room was empty.

Joanna tugged at the door handle; the section of glass slid open. She stepped inside, calling out to Jerry Eckridge. There was no reply. After calling out again, she crossed to the table and touched the crust of the pizza. It was cold. The beer was warm. A second glass stood near the edge of the opposite side of the table. Joanna sniffed the half-finger of amber-tinted liquid in it: bourbon.

Her unease increased. Unpleasant ripples moved over the back of her neck, and although she told herself she was being overimaginative, she couldn't shake the feeling that something was terribly wrong here. She went to an archway that led into a wide terra-cotta-floored hall and stood listening. Nothing moved or breathed in the house.

As she retraced her steps to the low table, she saw a cordless phone receiver lying on one of the couch cushions near where the pizza eater would have been sitting. That suggested one possible explanation: Jerry had been having his meal, received a phone call—probably from Adam, who had said he would keep trying to alert him to the problem with the Van Gogh—and gone tearing back to San Francisco. There had been no answer to Adam's earlier repeated calls to the ranch, which was why he'd asked Joanna to check on Jerry, but they could very well have connected in the interim. Another explanation was that Jerry had had a visitor—hence the glass of bourbon—and gone somewhere with him or her.

Fine, good. But it was still odd that he'd gone off without turning off the lights or locking the sliding door. And what about the car that had run her off the driveway?

She looked at the archway again. The feeling of something wrong intensified. But she could not bring herself to search the rest of the house.

Finally she picked up the receiver and flicked the talk switch. She ought to report the hit-and-run to the sheriff's department. While they were here they could look around, determine whether her fears about Jerry were justified. But would they search the premises merely because she suspected something was amiss?

You're getting ahead of yourself, she thought. Why don't you call Adam, see if he's contacted Jerry?

But when Adam answered his phone, the first thing he said was, "Have you had any luck locating Eckridge?"

"That was what I was calling to ask you. I'm at his ranch. It looks as if he had a phone call or a visitor and went off in a hurry—leaving the lights on and the door unlocked. And, Adam, someone ran me off the driveway on my way in here."

"Are you okay?"

"A little shaken up is all. The car's wrecked, though. And now that I know you haven't been in touch with Jerry, I'm sure something's wrong here. I'm going to call the sheriff's department."

"Good. I'm on my way."

She flicked the talk button, punched out 911. The dispatcher took down the particulars and told her to stay there; it would take at least fifteen minutes for a unit to reach the scene. Joanna dropped the receiver onto the couch and moved toward the glass door. She would feel more comfortable waiting outside.

When she reached the front of the house she crossed to the sedan and leaned against its rear flank. The night had grown cold; the wind had kicked up again. She thought of returning to shelter but rejected the idea almost at once.

Her neck and arms were hurting again. Was this what the ambulance chasers called whiplash? There was a tingling all the way down to her fingers. She stretched her arm back, trying to ease the discomfort.

Her hand touched the car's trunk. Its lid moved slightly. Unlatched.

She stepped around to the rear bumper and looked at the lid. No, she thought, don't do it. And then she did it anyway. Grasped the lid's edge, raised it.

An inside light flashed on. It shone down on Jerry Eckridge's blank eyes and bloodless features.

NINETEEN

ECKRIDGE HAD BEEN SHOT twice in the back with a small-caliber handgun, the sheriff's investigator later told her. The first pair of deputies had arrived while Joanna—immobilized by shock—was still staring down at Jerry's fetally curled body. They immediately radioed for backup. The call brought out, among others, a man named Lennon who attempted to question her, then had her sit in his official car until she was more coherent. The deputies entered the house and found bloodstains that indicated Eckridge had been killed in the terra-cotta-floored hallway, then wrapped in a blanket that now lay under his body in the trunk, and dragged outside to the car.

"What we think is that somebody came to see him," Lennon said. "Eckridge was on his way down the hall to show him to the door when he was shot. After the perpetrator stuffed him in the trunk, he was probably going to go back inside, clean up, then get rid of the body. But he heard you coming down the driveway, panicked, and drove off. That's why anything you can remember about the car is important."

It was an hour and a half later; they were in Lennon's office at the sheriff's department substation on Highway 12. The investigator—a stocky man with unruly gray hair and a handlebar mustache—was being excessively solicitous of Joanna. She suspected it stemmed not so much from real sympathy as from a desire to keep her cooperating. Lennon had told her right out that he was aware of her son's "problem" and hoped Eckridge's murder wasn't "part of it." When she'd responded straightforwardly—admitting

that there was a tenuous connection between the two kill-
ings but insisting on E.J.'s innocence of either—the investigator had seemed relieved, and began treating her with
extreme courtesy. Since they'd arrived at the substation he
had sent out for coffee, apologized for tape-recording their
conversation, asked if her chair was comfortable, and com-
plimented her twice on her calm handling of the situation.

"Most women would have been in hysterics when their car
was forced into the ditch," he said now.

Joanna—who disliked statements beginning with "most
women (men/children)"—chose not to respond to that. She
said, "As I told you back at the Eckridge place, I don't remember a thing about the car, except that it seemed fairly
large."

"Large as Eckridge's T-bird?"

"Possibly."

"What about the color?"

"It was dusk; everything looks gray at dusk."

"Everything looks *shades* of gray. Think: dark gray, light
gray, in between?"

She closed her eyes, pictured the headlights moving toward her. "Light gray."

The door to the office opened, and a deputy came in with
cardboard cups of coffee. Lennon waited until he had gone
before resuming.

"Let's go over all this one more time," he said. "You
went to the Eckridge place because this Adam Hawthorne
asked you to check up on him—"

They went over it one more time. Then they went over
what had happened after she'd arrived there. They talked
some more about the Van Gogh, the auction, Parducci's
murder, the revelation that the painting had been stolen.
The only part of it she left out was that pertaining to Davis
Deane; the old man could not have had anything to do with
Eckridge's murder, and she was still inclined to shield him.
Besides, she'd concluded that it was mere coincidence that

they'd both been run off the road. Finally Lennon told her she could go. He would be in touch. He thanked her very much for her cooperation.

But now Joanna had a question of her own. As she stood, she said, "Detective Lennon, you mentioned my son. Has he been arrested yet?"

"No, Mrs. Stark. There hasn't been a sign of him since his motorcycle turned up in that park-and-ride lot across from Ford's Café."

"Since I've cooperated with you, will you let me know if you hear anything about E.J.?"

"I'll be glad to."

She left the office, half-expecting to see Adam waiting there. He'd intended to go to the Eckridge ranch; one of the deputies would have told him where she'd been taken.

But instead she found Sally Jane, obviously alerted to what had happened by the police band radio in her van. "There you are!" she said. "I've come to drive you home—and get an interview."

"Oh shit."

"Thanks a lot."

"Sorry. It's just that I've been talking for hours, and I'm too tired to give you anything coherent."

"Leave that to me; I'll make it make sense." Sally Jane steered her toward the exit.

Joanna's Fiat had been impounded by the sheriff's department, to be checked for paint scrapings from the other car. Even if it hadn't been, it was undrivable. She had no way home, except for the lift in a patrol car that Lennon had earlier promised and then seemed to have forgotten.

She went willingly with Sally Jane, for once glad to be the cared-for, rather than the caretaker.

"So why do you think Eckridge was shot?" Sally Jane asked.

Joanna shrugged. They were sitting in the reporter's van in front of the newspaper offices. Her friend had missed the deadline for the early-week edition, but she planned to give her exclusive interview with Joanna to the San Francisco *Chronicle*, for which she also worked as a stringer.

"All comes back to that painting," Sally Jane said. "Eckridge bought it from somebody—maybe the person who stole it originally. Whoever that was might have killed him to keep him from telling."

"The painting was stolen right after World War One. The thief would be too old to care now, much less to shoot Jerry, drag his body outside, and hoist it into the trunk."

"Well, somebody cared."

"Maybe there's no connection. Maybe his wife shot him. They *were* getting divorced." When she looked at Sally Jane, she saw a speculative gleam in her eyes. "No," she added quickly, "I was just kidding."

"Well, I still think that painting's at the root of all this. And the other one, *The Vineyard at Marmande*. That brings us to Davis Deane—"

"I told you anything about him is off the record."

Sally Jane looked injured. "I wouldn't violate a confidence. And I don't want to hurt the old man, either. I'll leave him out of it until we know exactly how he's involved. But he's got to be—and he's got to have that painting. But *where*?"

Joanna had an idea, but she wasn't ready to share it yet. Instead of answering, she asked, "Why did you send me to Deane in the first place? I took it to mean he has some knowledge of art collecting."

"I've always assumed he does."

"But why?"

Sally Jane frowned, her wide mouth pulling downward. "I'm not sure. You know how you make these assumptions—hear something at some point, store it away, forget it. But the general impression's still there. I do know that when I tried to interview him, he steered me away from my questions about artistic interests. Pointedly, in fact.''

"Why did you want to interview him in the first place?"

"Had a human interest piece in mind. How a man who had everything ended up in his position. Tie it in with the homeless problem—this could happen to any of us, that sort of stuff."

Joanna nodded, feeling weary and depressed.

"You ought to look into that right away," Sally Jane said.

"Into what?"

"Deane. Where he's got that painting."

"Oh, right."

"Slow on the uptake tonight, Jo. Maybe you should get some sleep—"

"Quiet a second. Let me think."

Sally Jane fidgeted. Fifteen seconds proved to be her limit. "What are you—"

Joanna silenced her again. "Why don't you drop me at Karla Perilli's? I need to talk to her, and that'll give you time to do your story. Come back and pick me up when you're finished."

IT WAS LONG after midnight; Karla had been sleeping. When she saw Joanna at the door she registered shock, jumping to the conclusion that she'd come with bad news about Davis Deane. After Joanna reassured her, she became annoyed and almost didn't let her inside. Finally, however, they were settled in deeply cushioned easy chairs in Karla's cozy living room behind her company's offices, where Joanna once again related the story of the two Van Goghs.

By way of concluding she said, "My suspicion is that your great-grandfather sold *Flowers along the Rhone* some twenty-five years ago to Jerry Eckridge. I also suspect he's got the sister painting hidden at the resort. Do you know if he served in the First World War?"

"He didn't. Davis had asthma as a child. Even though it never has bothered him as an adult, it was enough of a medical history to keep him out of the service. I know that because my grandmother used to tell me how proud he was that his son was a pilot in World War Two."

"Then he probably wasn't the one who stole the Van Goghs, but it's a good possibility he knows who did. That knowledge can be dangerous to him."

Karla drew her legs up into her chair, and tucked her turquoise bathrobe around her bare feet. "You really think his accident is related to all this?"

"If what he said about the other truck forcing him off the road is true, it could be."

The younger woman didn't respond for a moment. Joanna waited, studying her. Karla obviously hadn't been sleeping any better than she had: There was a blueish tinge to the pale skin under her eyes, and their lids were reddened. After a moment she sighed. "All right. What can I do to help him?"

"Do you have keys to the hotel at the resort?"

"God, no. Like I told you the other day, I'm lucky I've gotten as far as the porch of Davis's cabin."

"Well, that doesn't matter. There's a burglar alarm on the courtyard, but it's an old one, and I know how to disarm it. What I need from you is your written permission to go onto the property and remove certain things."

"Can I give that?"

"You're his next of kin, and he's unable to. I think it would stand up in court. But I doubt it'll ever come to that; I just want it in writing in case something goes wrong."

"All right. What shall I authorize you to remove?"

"Artworks. Paintings, specifically. And better say papers, too. Documents, records. He keeps all his personal files in the area that's protected by the alarm. There might be something helpful in them."

Karla got up and moved toward the door to her office.
"When are you going there?"

"Right away."

"Alone?"

Joanna thought of her lack of a car, and of the police
band radio in Sally Jane's van.

"No," she said. "I'm taking a friend."

"DID YOU GET IT?" Sally Jane asked anxiously.

"Almost."

"Be careful you don't electrocute yourself."

"I know what I'm doing. I could do this in my sleep!"

"Well, just be careful. Don't fall."

Joanna bit back a sarcastic reply and turned her attention to the second to last screw on the outside alarm box.
Sally Jane had pulled the van back into the trees next to the
hotel's walled courtyard; Joanna was standing on its roof,
from where she could just reach the box. She didn't feel as
confident as she sounded; in spite of the flashlight Sally
Jane held, it was dark, and she was operating at an awkward angle.

In the van below her a dispatcher's voice said, *"Twenty-
one-two Adam Santa Rosa, I've got an eleven-eighty-two for
you, College and Slater."*

Joanna loosened the screw, began on the last one.

"Go ahead," the dispatcher said.

"Thanks," she muttered.

*"Twenty-one-six Charles, comes back clear on your
Chrysler LeBaron, expiration one-nine-ninety. VRO is Lana
Waite, fifteen-oh-eighty Encina Court, Sebastopol. Too
bad, that description would have been real close. One-
Adam, your traffic."*

The screwdriver slipped from Joanna's hand and clanged
onto the van roof. She squatted down, feeling for it.

"All available units vicinity Boyes Boulevard and Pine, I've got a four-fifteen, repeat, a four-fifteen, Boyes Boulevard and Pine."

"At least the SO's being kept busy," Sally Jane said. "They won't come by here and bother us."

Joanna located the screwdriver. "What's a four-fifteen?"

"Disturbance. Probably a bar brawl, or something to do with drugs."

Joanna turned her attention back to the screw. In spite of the so-called weatherproof cover on the box, years of damp had caused a good deal of corrosion. She applied more pressure, and the screw began to turn.

"I didn't copy all that... Seventeen-one-seven, I need you to clear for an eleven-eighty, Stony Point and Hearn... Seventeen-forty-four, what's your ETA for the county line?"

Joanna removed the cover on the box. "Shine that light closer, will you?" Sally Jane complied. She studied the wires inside. "Just as I thought—a piece of cake."

Sally Jane lowered the flashlight. "No," Joanna said, "keep that where you had it. If I screw up now, the alarm'll go off for sure."

A squawk from the radio: *"Proceed with caution, repeat—"*

"Right," Joanna said. Then she concentrated on the box in front of her, keeping her touch light, working from memory. Funny how things you'd done routinely years before came back to you....

"SA sixty, all units, citizens reporting vehicle proceeding north on one-oh-one vicinity Hamilton Air Force Base containing marijuana plants in rear seat, white Toyota Tercel, VIN one GDJ three-two-six—"

"How're you doing?"

"Okay so far." A couple more delicate connections to sever...

"All available units vicinity Boyes Boulevard and Pine, Code three urgent, eleven-ninety-nine, officer needs assistance, repeat—"

"Some bar brawl!" Sally Jane said. "I hope you realize I may be missing a good story."

Joanna blocked out both the sound of the radio and her friend's voice. Move slowly, she told herself. Don't hurry.

The last connecting wire slipped free. She let out a sigh, dropped into a crouch, easing her strained muscles.

"You got it?" Sally Jane asked.

"I got it. What I'm going to do now is break some glass, go down into the courtyard through the roof. The front door is chained from the outside, so I'll have to boost the stuff up here to you."

"Just whistle. And don't cut yourself."

"Yes, Mom."

She pulled herself up onto the sharply canting top section of the wall, next to the greenhouse roof. The sore muscles in her neck and arm gave a protesting twinge. She balanced there, took off her jacket, and wrapped it around her hand. Then she whacked hard at the section of roof in front of her. Several panes shattered, glass raining inward. The crossbeams between them were rotten; most fell too, or hung downward, connected by mere slivers of wood. She removed what shards remained in the weak frame until the space was large enough to allow her to pass.

"I'm going inside now," she said to Sally Jane.

"Good luck."

She slid to the edge of the canting wall and lowered herself through the space she'd cleared, dangling from her hands and then dropping to the tiled floor below. The soles of her shoes smacked down loudly; shards of glass crunched. A wide swath of moonlight lay over the courtyard at the end nearest the hotel. Joanna moved toward it, kicking aside pieces of broken roof beam.

The first obstacle, she thought, would be the doors to the interior. Their panes were heavy old beveled glass; something in her shrank from shattering them. But she remembered locking them as she'd left the courtyard on Friday....

When she tested the doorhandle, however, it turned. Someone had been here since her visit.

Who? she wondered. The man who had chased her into the ravine? She didn't think there had been enough time for him to enter the hotel before she'd heard his truck drive away. But she'd been panicked, and her sense of timing might have been skewed.

She raised her flashlight, shone it around the room beyond the doors. Nothing had changed; the painting in the style of Degas still hung above the mantel. She crossed and examined it thoroughly, looking for evidence of overpainting or other tampering. There was none; the painting was a genuine mediocre effort of an inferior artist. She hadn't really expected otherwise; the canvases she was interested in were the ones hanging in the third-floor hallway, where the air was dry and suitable for storing a valuable work.

She crossed the lobby and hurried up the stairs, bypassing the second floor. Moonlight spilled through the unboarded windows of the third story, silvering the floral pattern of the worn rug in the hall. The branches of a tree tapped restlessly against one corner of the building; glass rattled in its panes. Joanna paused at the top of the stairs. She thought she heard another, more irregular noise beneath those generated by the wind.

A movement—quick and scurrying. Mice or rats? Squirrels would find this old building a haven. Raccoons might have taken up residence in the eaves.

She continued to listen. The sound came again. No, she told herself, it could not have been made by anything human.

She crossed to the painting that hung closest, removed it from its hook, examined it with care. Disappointed, she re-

placed it, went on to the second, third, and fourth. All were
of the same quality as that downstairs. None of the clever
techniques that thieves use to disguise canvases had been
employed.

She didn't remember having seen any other paintings on
Friday, but she made her way through the entire third floor
again, then descended to the second. For a moment she
considered searching there, too, but her recollection of previously doing so was clear; these rooms had been stripped
even of light fixtures. Finally she returned to the courtyard
and removed Deane's boxes of papers from the small room
behind the latticework at the far end of the pool.

She called to Sally Jane and told her she was ready to
boost the boxes up to her. Her friend climbed on the wall to
help. At the last minute Joanna remembered the box she'd
hidden under the stairs and made a trip back to the lobby to
fetch it. When she'd handed it up, she hesitated beside the
debris-filled pool, wondering whether she had missed any
conceivable hiding place for *The Vineyard at Marmande*.
She could search again, but her watch showed three-thirty.
Besides, if she hadn't found the painting, it would remain
safe until Deane was well enough to tell her where it was.

As she grasped Sally Jane's extended hands and wriggled
up through the opening in the roof, the radio in the van
crackled. The dispatcher's voice said, *"Ten-four, over and
out."*

TWENTY

JOANNA SAID, "I think I've found the connection!"

Adam took off his glasses and pinched the bridge of his nose. "Thank God."

It was close to five in the morning. They were in the living room of Joanna's house, where Adam had been waiting when she and Sally Jane returned. Deane's papers were arranged in piles on the floor, sofa, and tables. Sally Jane had just gone to the kitchen to brew more coffee.

"So what is it?" he added.

"Jerry Eckridge's ranch used to belong to Davis Deane. He bought it from Deane without the aid of a real estate broker in July of nineteen-sixty-three."

"So?"

"Look." She knee-walked from where she sat on the floor to his chair, unceremoniously pushing aside Herman, who slept between two stacks of documents. "Here're the escrow papers, signed by both of them. The space for the agent's signature is blank."

"I don't see why that's important."

"It means they knew one another personally, around the time that Jerry bought the Van Gogh."

"Joanna." Adam spoke with the patience of one who has been sorely tried. "That proves nothing."

"I didn't say it *proved* a thing. But they had dealings around the time that Deane was liquidating his assets and Jerry was starting an art collection. If Deane had *Flowers* in his possession, he might have sold it to Jerry in order to raise additional cash."

Adam sighed.

"Yes," she agreed, "it sounds farfetched. But that's only because we don't have all the information yet." She dropped the escrow papers on the floor beside her and sat back on her heels, staring up at him. Adam looked bone-tired, and she couldn't blame him; he'd had as little sleep as she in the last few days. But he had as much at stake in this as she did—more, because tracing the Van Gogh was directly related to his problem while only tangentially related to Parducci's murder and E.J.'s disappearance. She continued staring, as if the intensity of her gaze might galvanize him.

After a moment he smiled and set his glasses on the end table. "Where do you get your energy?"

"I'm running on reserves. Usually I'm pretty lazy. The word *indolent* has been bandied about. But this—" She put her hands on his knee and grasped it hard, suddenly afraid she might be losing him. "We're on to something here, Adam. It's important. I know it is."

The harsh, weary lines on his face softened. "I'll take your word for it." He leaned forward and cupped her face in his hands. For a moment their eyes met and held. Then he tilted his head and touched his lips to hers.

Her first instinct was to pull back, but surprise and—quickly—pleasure held her there. She brought her hand up to cover one of his, savoring that subtle alteration of perspective that happens once in a relationship, when a friend crosses the boundary into intimacy and everything is forever altered....

"Think you need a new coffee maker," Sally Jane's voice announced. "Heating element's—oops!"

Joanna jerked back on her heels. Adam sighed.

"Sorry about that." The reporter set the glass pot on a trivet on the table. "Should I leave and come back later?"

"There's no going back," Adam said, with more humor than Joanna was sure he felt. "Besides," he added, eyes on her face, "there'll be plenty of time for us later."

Her cheeks were hot. Good God, she thought crossly, forty-three years old, and I'm blushing like a teenager caught kissing her first date!

Sally Jane grinned smugly at her; Joanna knew why. In spite of her determinedly single state, her friend was always intent on grouping everyone else into couples. Sally Jane had had a happy marriage that ended when her husband was killed in an accident years ago; she was certain she'd never find such wedded bliss again, but insistent that all those she cared about should enjoy it.

"Well, as I started to say, the coffee maker's going kaput. You find anything while I was out there—besides each other?"

Joanna rolled her eyes at her, then explained about Deane's sale of the Glen Ellen property to Eckridge.

Sally Jane's reaction was the same as Adam's. "So?"

Joanna said, "Out of context, it means very little. But it might narrow down the date of sale of that painting. If only I knew—"

"What?"

She shrugged. "More about Deane, maybe. He doesn't strike me as your typical receiver of stolen property, so there has to be some other reason he had those paintings—"

Adam said, "Are you sure he did?"

"He must have at least had *The Vineyard at Marmande*."

He nodded.

Sally Jane said, "You know, Deane was a big man in this valley once. Big men get written up in small-town papers all the time. Why don't you check our microfilms?"

"Can you get us into the offices at this hour?"

"Like all trusted and esteemed employees, I have a key to the building."

THE MICROFILM MACHINE gave off a murky glow in the darkened newspaper library. As she'd begun looking through the first reel for the period 1955–1965—an arbitrary choice based on the manner the films were stored—Joanna had commented to Adam that she felt as if they were trapped in a hermetically sealed underwater cavern. Then she'd become oblivious to her surroundings, caught up in the events of a simpler, more gentle time—before man had walked on the moon and computers had come into the home; before the country had been torn apart by an undeclared war; before anyone had ever heard of AIDS or crack, and Coke was still something you bought for a quarter from a machine.

In 1957 the Pat Boone movie *April Love* had drawn record crowds at the Sebastiani Theater. The next year Boone's rival, Elvis Presley, had gone into the army and the furor over the "young punk" from Memphis had largely died down, although Mrs. Ella Marchetti of El Verano told the paper's inquiring reporter that she still considered Presley a "dangerous influence on our impressionable youth." The 1959 Harvest Festival had been a great success. In 1960 the town council had become alarmed over the growing incidence of juvenile crime. Angry letters to the editor stated that parents should control their offspring; letters from the parents and offsprings themselves protested the lack of organized acitivities in the town. What else, they asked, was there to do but hang out in the plaza and bowling alley?

Crime had definitely been on the upswing at the start of the new decade. Burglaries increased dramatically. One of the households hit was Robert Donatello's; in June of 1960 the vintner reported the loss of a collection of rare coins and several valuable paintings and objects of art. Acting police chief Davis Deane had called for an all-out investigation into crime in the city....

"Adam!" Joanna said.

He moved behind her and read the item over her shoulder while she reread it. The burglary of the Donatellos' eastside estate had occurred in the evening, on the servants' day off, while the family was at their summer home on Lake Tahoe. The burglars had apparently entered the property in a delivery truck and carted off their spoils through the main gates. Robert Donatello was quoted: "Everything was fully insured, of course. But money doesn't compensate for the loss in sentimental value. Some of those things had belonged to my family back in the old country." Davis Deane, a close friend of the vintner, had said, "This break-in at the home of one of our most prominent citizens is symptomatic of the crime wave that has hit this valley. The officers investigating the case will report directly to me."

"Paintings," Joanna said.

"And Deane as acting police chief. Why *acting*?"

Joanna rememberd the clipping in the box of Deane's mementoes. "A few months before this item ran, the chief died suddenly. Deane filled in while they hired a new one."

"Could Deane have engineered the theft himself and got his men to cover up?"

"Possibly. He was friendly with Donatello; he would have known the family was away and could have found out what night the servants had off. I'm going to keep scanning these films for something further on it." Joanna pressed the button on her machine and moved ahead.

For a few weeks the Donatello burglary remained in the news; Deane reported that the police were pursuing promising leads. Then there was nothing. Interest turned from the crime wave to the increase in summer tourism; to the fall grape harvest; to high-school football. A new police chief was hired in September; presumably the Donatello investigation was backburnered or merely overlooked in the confusion of the transition.

She scanned more quickly now, into the early months of 1961. The Deanes and Donatellos were mentioned numerous times in connection with social events and civic causes. In April of that year, the two friends were pictured together at the groundbreaking ceremonies for Donatello Vineyards' new multimillion-dollar facilities near Vineburg. Then in October an obituary for Deane's wife Bea appeared. After that only the Donatellos were mentioned in the paper.

What had happened, Joanna suspected, was that Deane had started his heavy drinking after losing Bea. Kept to himself, didn't tend to his business interests. By the time he'd realized everything was going down the tubes, it was too late to do anything except sell off his holdings piecemeal, until all he had left was Madrone Springs Resort.

But none of that explained what Karla Perelli had described as a falling-out between the two men.

Joanna reversed the film to the story of the winery groundbreaking and studied the picture of Deane and Donatello. They were clowning around, their hands on the ceremonial shovel. She read the accompanying article. After years of delays and difficulties with financing, it said, the project for the expanded facilities was finally going ahead. The construction would provide jobs for a hundred local workers; the facility itself would eventually employ an equal number...

"Years of delay," she said. "Difficulties with financing."

Still looking over her shoulder, Adam added, "And suddenly Donatello got capital—after the burglary of a lot of 'fully insured' objects of art."

"Not suddenly. But within the time it would take an insurance company to verify and pay off on the claim."

"No wonder former acting chief of police Deane played such a prominent role in the groundbreaking ceremonies."

Joanna wound the film back, replaced it in its container, and switched off the machine. "Not a pretty picture, is it?"

"Not if you care about old man Deane—and I think you do."

"That's the part that hurts, all right. I'm not sure where to go from here. My thinking's fuzzy. Coffee would help."

He held out his hand. "Let's go."

They passed through the editorial offices, waving to Sally Jane, who was at her desk, coffee and doughnuts to hand. The reporter started to join them, but her phone rang. As she snatched it up, Joanna said, "I'll call you later." She and Adam went out into the cool sweet-smelling dawn.

The streets were hushed; what few cars went by moved slowly, as if their drivers were still half asleep. Down the block a small crowd of commuters awaited the Greyhound to San Francisco.

"Let's go over to Stein's on Broadway," Joanna said. "They open early; the cops hang out there."

Adam nodded and they began walking toward the plaza, both with their hands thrust into their pockets, heads bowed. In spite of her preoccupation Joanna noticed and smiled wearily. A phrase her mother had been fond of popped into her head: *Two sides of the same coin.*

They halted at the corner to let a string of traffic go by. Joanna began thinking out loud, removing her hands from her pockets and using them to shape ideas. "Suppose that the two Van Goghs were stolen by Robert Donatello. No, that can't be; he's at least ten years younger than Deane, too young to have been in Paris after the war. Suppose they ended up in the Donatello family, then—in the 'old country,' as Robert said. Suppose that one of the European Donatellos stole them, or ordered them stolen, and Robert was aware of that when he inherited them.

"He wanted to raise capital to expand his winery. The paintings were the obvious way, but he didn't dare sell them because a dealer or auction house might recognize them and demand an explanation. While Donatello himself had done nothing illegal, the revelation about his family could be damaging, both to him personally and to the winery. I've noticed Donatello places a high value on his 'good name.'"

A van that had been waiting at the stop sign passed through the intersection. Adam touched her arm and they started across the street.

"Okay," she went on. "Donatello's friend Deane is acting chief of police. They fake a burglary. Donatello's well insured—maybe overinsured. Deane makes sure the investigation doesn't go too deep, expedites the insurance settlement. Donatello gets his money and builds his winery."

"And the paintings?"

"They were probably the only things 'stolen' that Donatello couldn't sell. The other art objects and the coin collection might have brought additional cash from dealers who wouldn't ask too many questions. But Donatello had to keep the Van Goghs. He wouldn't have wanted to destroy them; they were too valuable, and there was the chance he might find a way to convert them to cash in the future. I think he entrusted them to Deane."

"Why not just take them back to his house after the investigation was shelved?"

"I know if *I* were faking a burglary and making a false insurance claim, I wouldn't keep the supposedly stolen goods on the premises—not for a long time afterward, if ever."

"That's reasonable."

"All right. Deane and Donatello had a falling-out not long after that. I don't know why; neither does Deane's great-granddaughter. But it was a bad one. Maybe Donatello refused to bail Deane out of his financial troubles. Maybe Deane had second thoughts about the theft and wanted to go to the police. Maybe it was strictly a family matter—there was a link by marriage. But whatever happened, Deane eventually sold *Flowers along the Rhone* to Jerry Eckridge, without Donatello's knowledge or permission."

They stopped at the town's main intersection, where Broadway dead-ends at the plaza. Adam displayed no inclination to keep walking. Joanna was busy ordering her thoughts.

After a moment she went on. "Twenty-five years passed. Eckridge was in financial trouble, just as Deane had been when he sold him *Flowers*. Jerry knew nothing of the painting's shady past. Or maybe he suspected something wasn't quite right, but he knew he had clear title to it, so he put it up for auction. Because of the inflated prices Van Goghs have been bringing, there was worldwide publicity. That worried someone; if an expert, like your Mr. Eschler, came out of the woodwork, it could ruin everyone connected with that painting. But if the painting disappeared before it could be auctioned—if a theft were arranged, nothing would ever have to come out."

"And so someone hired Parducci."

"Yes."

"And killed him when the theft didn't come off. And killed Jerry to keep him silent about where he'd acquired the painting."

"No, that can't be." Joanna stared across the street at the plaza, trying to put her finger on what was wrong. The eight-acre town square lay cloaked in early-morning shadow; the grass was sheened with dew; even the ducks still nested under the bushes by the pond. In front of city hall, the detritus of last night's political rally lay on the U-shaped driveway; banners and posters stirred in the light breeze.

"What's wrong?" Adam asked.

She shook her head, kept staring at the fluttering strips of red and blue, kept piecing everything together. Then she turned abruptly and began walking back toward where Adam's car was parked.

He fell into step beside her. "Where are we going?"

"To the sheriff's department. And then to my son's winery. On the way I'll fill you in about Antony Parducci and me."

TWENTY-ONE

ADAM PULLED his Mercedes onto the shoulder of Highway 12 some hundred yards away from the entrance to Stark Vineyards. Joanna leaned forward, one hand on the dashboard, staring at the driveway. It was at least five minutes before Joe's red truck appeared, weaving around the potholes. It paused for traffic to clear, then turned toward town. As it passed them, she caught a glimpse of his face: tense and preoccupied, obviously worried about her telephone request that he meet her at her house.

When the truck was out of sight, she said, "Let's go."

Adam started the car and drove down the shoulder and into the winery.

The only vehicle in the parking area was the rattletrap company pickup. Adam pulled the Mercedes behind it and got out. Joanna remained in the car for a moment, looking at the truck. Then she nodded to herself and fished in her bag for the winery keys that E.J. had proudly presented her only days before. When she joined Adam at the big front doors, he scrutinized her face and said, "You okay?"

"As well as can be expected." She inserted the key in the lock; it turned with difficulty. When the door swung open, the familiar musty wine smell enveloped her. Usually it was an odor that gave pleasure; this morning it made her vaguely nauseated.

She entered the tasting room, felt to the right of the door for a switch. The lights came on—garish fluorescents, unsuited to the cavernlike chamber. Joanna blinked.

Very little appeared to have been done with the room since the day she had brought the picnic lunch. The floor was clean, and some of the mold had been scraped from the walls, but cartons were still piled helter-skelter. In one corner lay a heap of debris: collapsed boxes, impossibly moldy wine casks, rags, crumbled newspaper, broken glass.

Adam closed the door and locked it. "You want to start here?" he asked.

"No, I don't think this is where he'd keep it." She went on through the doors at the rear of the room into the winery proper. Oaken casks lay on racks on either side of a central aisle; beyond them tall wooden vats hulked in the shadows. It was cooler and darker there, the musty wine smell more acute. Joanna's stomach lurched and she felt a tightness in her throat.

She continued past the casks to a door at the far right, pushed it open, and stepped into the makeshift living quarters. They too were full of unpacked boxes. An open suitcase half full of clothing lay on the floor next to a futon covered with plaid flannel sheets. The sheets were badly rumpled, the pillow twisted into segments, as if someone had tried to strangle it. Although E.J. had moved his backpack and sleeping bag to the winery on the morning the real estate agent had turned over the keys, they were nowhere in sight.

Joanna gave the room a cursory examination and went into the lab. The crates of equipment stood exactly as they had on Saturday night. The card table and three chairs remained in place. Even the coffee mug that she'd drunk from stood in front of the chair she'd occupied; its contents were filmed with dust.

She said to Adam, "This is where I think it'll be."

He didn't ask why, just began helping her search. They moved through the heavy crates with calm deliberation. What they were seeking was wedged behind a large carton in one corner.

Joanna's stomach lurched again as she looked down at the small newspaper-wrapped package. She'd known it would be here, but at some level she'd hoped to be proven wrong. When she glanced back at Adam, he made a small sound—dismay? Commiseration? She lifted the package, took it to the card table, ripped the newspaper wrappings free.

The painting was unprepossessing—drab, acutally: a scene of Flemish peasants cavorting around a keg of beer in a country garden. For a moment Joanna flashed back to the first time she'd seen it, in London, when her art dealer friend had unveiled it and proclaimed, "So—*There Hangs the Knife*." It wasn't a genuine masterpiece, and close to a year ago, when she'd hung it in her front hall, she'd changed its name to *Stark's Dark Star*.

The painting had hung there to warn her against indulging in foolhardy, self-serving schemes. Now it had come to symbolize another person's folly.

Adam came up behind her, placed his hands on her shoulders. She leaned back against him, grateful for the solidity and warmth.

"There's your proof," he said. "Now we wait. And you do what you have to."

The fifteen minutes they had to wait were among the longest of Joanna's life. She was so tired she was afraid her wits might not sustain her through the unpleasant confrontation ahead. Her nerves were none too steady, either—set on edge by a combination of exhaustion and the cumulative shock of finding two dead men in a mere twenty-four hours. As the minutes strung out, she found herself dreading Joe's arrival, so much so that when the sound of an engine alerted her, she started violently.

She glanced tensely at Adam as footsteps came along the path beyond the lab's outside door. Seconds later a key rattled in the lock. When Joe entered, he didn't appear to see them at first. His eyes were drawn to where *Dark Star* lay on the table.

He shut the door and pocketed his keys in slow motion. Only then did he look at Joanna. "All right," he said stiffly, "what's this about? I went to your place, and you weren't home. What're you doing here?"

"Searching for my property." She motioned at the painting.

"What is that, anyway?"

"You know, Joe."

"I've never seen it before in my life."

"You've seen it many times, in my front hallway. And you saw it before you hid it over there."

His eyes followed her outflung hand, then came back to the painting. For a moment she thought he would keep running his bluff, but then his shoulders slumped and he crossed to one of the chairs and sat down heavily. "You didn't have to resort to tricks to get me out of here," he said.

"If I'd just asked you for the painting, would you have given it to me?"

"...I don't know."

"Joe, I want you to tell me where E.J. is—and if he's all right."

"Of course he's all right. I found him a safe place to stay until I could...decide what to do about all this. No point in him being thrown into jail for something he didn't do."

"Kind of you."

Anger flickered in his eyes. "Look don't start on me, okay? I *know* I'm a bastard—I don't need you to remind me." Then his gaze moved to Adam. "Who's he? A cop?"

"Adam Hawthorne. His auction house sold the Van Gogh."

"The man who brought the whole thing tumbling down."

"Don't blame him. What's happened was set in motion more than twenty-five years ago."

"Well, don't blame me, either. That was old Robert's doing. I wasn't even born then."

"But this *was* your doing. You could have said no."

"That shows what you know about families like mine."

She bit back a tart reply, realizing she would get nowhere by antagonizing him. And, in truth, there was some valid- ity to what he'd said. She'd chosen to withdraw from her own family at an early age; even with David and E.J. she'd never fully succeeded in establishing one. What did she really know about the dynamics of families?

From behind her Adam said, "Look, Joanna, why don't we sit down, too? No point in standing around—we've got a lot to talk about." It was the same mild, conciliatory tone he'd surprised her with in the tense meeting at the auction house during the early hours of Saturday morning. His ap- proach had worked then, would probably work now. She sat.

Her doing so had an immediate calming effect on Joe. He turned, leaning his forearms on the table, and met her eyes. "Jo, for whatever it's worth, I'm sorry."

"I know." She watched Adam pick up one of the chairs and reposition it between the table and the outside door—in case, she knew—Joe decided to bolt. She doubted he would, though. She sensed resignation in him—relief, too. Joe was a decent man; the burden of guilt he was carrying had to be a heavy one.

She said, "Whose idea was it to hire Parducci to arrange the theft of the Van Gogh—your grandfather's, or Veronica's?"

"His, of course. Ronnie didn't even know until every- thing started to fall apart. Not that it would have bothered her that it was illegal or unethical. He just didn't want any- thing to take her mind off campaigning. Ronnie's my grandfather's last great hope, after our parents were killed and I turned out to be a piss-poor excuse for the heir he thought would take the political world by storm."

"I'll concede that what your grandfather did might have had a backlash on Ronnie's reputation. But most voters re- alize you can't blame the children for their parents'—or grandparents'—transgressions. Besides, it might not even have come out until long after the election.''

"Grandfather wasn't willing to chance that. You see, our family has spent generations living down the misdeeds of our black sheep. Donatellos have been up to their necks in scandal and crime since the Roman Empire; the respectable members of the family just keep rising above it all, only to fall again. The branch that settled in California left Italy in order to start fresh, but temptation followed in the form of those stolen paintings. Something corrupt in the blood seems to respond to the opportunity for underhanded dealings, I guess.''

"So your grandfather saw this as history repeating itself?''

"Yes, and his pride wouldn't permit him to risk it happening.''

"But why, if you're such a 'piss-poor excuse,' as you put it, did he bring you in on it?''

"He had to. Parducci wanted something more than money to undertake the job. I was the only one who could supply it.''

"The keys to my house.''

"Right.''

"Joe, why would you do a thing like that to me? You and E.J. had talked about Parducci; obviously you knew he'd tried to kill me before—''

"I didn't know he was the one who'd asked for the keys. I gave them to my grandfather.''

"How on earth did he explain wanting them?''

"He said he had a surprise for E.J. Something to celebrate him taking possession of the winery, to reassure him that he wasn't angry at him for hiring me away from the family business.''

"And you *believed* that?''

"You believe what you want to, I guess.''

"Let's backtrack a minute. How do you suppose Parducci knew you were in a position to get hold of keys to my house?"

"I don't know, but I've got the idea he's been keeping tabs on you and E.J. It turns out he knew all about him buying this winery, for instance."

It wasn't surprising, Joanna thought. Parducci had known where they lived, been in the house once, a year and a half before. With that information as a basis, he could have found out many things. "Go on."

"Grandfather asked for the keys when he came here the day you brought the picnic. He'd been pleasant to you and E.J., so I bought his story and gave them to him, and made sure you wouldn't be going home for a while. We met in town about forty minutes later. He had the painting with him." Joe motioned at *Dark Star*.

"How did he explain that?"

"It was part of the surprise, he said. Last night he admitted that Parducci had gone to your house with him, seen the painting, and said it was an extraordinary stroke of luck. He also saw the keys on E.J.'s ring that were tagged as belonging to the city apartment, and made Grandfather have them copied."

Another stroke of luck for him, Joanna thought. Parducci had also visited Rex's building on his last trip to San Francisco. "What made you decide to hide the painting at Madrone Springs Resort?" she asked.

Joe looked surprised. "You recognized me?"

"Not then. But this morning when I started putting all this together, I remembered the newspaper-wrapped package the man who chased me was carrying. And I realized that the pickup I'd seen pulled under the trees could have been the winery's."

"Funny, the only reason I took it was that E.J.'s bike was blocking mine. He came storming up here after the two of you had that fight, and we sat up talking all night. What he told me—about the matchbook and the missing painting and your fear that Parducci was trying to lure you out and kill you—proved my grandfather's story was all a lie. I was afraid E.J. would find the painting here and realize my part in it, so when he finally went to sleep I thought of the resort. Karla'd been talking about it since she'd started spending time there with Mr. Deane, and she'd called to say he'd had an accident and was in the hospital. It struck me as the ideal place to hide the painting until I could confront my grandfather.''

"Why didn't you leave it there, then? You had the keys—you took them from the padlock after you scared me into the ravine.''

"I started to, but then I realized I didn't know if you had access to another set. And I wasn't sure exactly what your relationship to Deane was. So I just brought the painting back here.''

"Joe, did you have anything to do with Davis Deane being run off the road?''

"I did not.''

She believed him.

Adam said, "What I'd like to know is why Parducci went to such elaborate lengths. He had keys to your house. If he intended to kill you—and it's safe to assume he did—why didn't he just do it there, make it look as if you'd surprised a burglar?''

"That would have been too simple for him," Joanna said. "Parducci had a sadistic flair for the dramatic. He wanted me to know he was alive, to worry, and to go after him one more time. And he knew that leaving the matchbook from the Greenbank Hotel would do just that. No wonder he was delighted at finding I still had *Dark Star*; it only made the game that much more elaborate.''

Joe sighed and leaned forward, resting his face on his folded arms.

"What do you suppose went wrong, Joe?" Joanna asked. "Why was Parducci killed?"

He flinched and didn't reply.

"Are you aware that your grandfather killed Jerry Eckridge, the former owner of the Van Gogh?" she added.

He raised his head, features twisted in anguish. After a moment he nodded. "He—" His voice cracked. He cleared his throat and began again. "He came here last night in a panic. I've never seen him that way before. He admitted everything about Parducci. He told me he'd killed Eckridge because he insisted he was going to reveal where he'd gotten the Van Gogh. My grandfather offered him a lot of money—enough to salvage his shipping line—but Eckridge said that when the whole story came out, the Van Gogh would be even more valuable, and then he'd put it up for auction again. So my grandfather shot him."

"With premeditation."

"He didn't intend—"

"He took a gun with him."

"...Yes." Joe was silent for a moment. "Anyway, he told me about trying to tidy up. That was how he put it—'tidy up.' And that a car had come along and he'd run it off the driveway. He wanted me to go up there and finish what he'd started. I refused. I'd done enough for him. He left in a terrible state."

"Where is he now?"

Joe shrugged. "At home, probably. By now he's manufacturing some alibi. He was supposed to be at Ronnie's rally at the plaza last night; he's probably got a dozen people to swear he was there."

Joanna sighed and looked at Adam. He pointed at his watch.

She said to Joe, "You have to turn him in. You can't let him get away with this."

"Don't you think I know that? But he'll never admit to it all again, and it'll be his word against mine."

"Call him up, get him over here."

"What? I told you, he'll never confess again. Especially not in front of the two of you."

"Of course not. But I do think he'll come, if you tell him you've found somebody who saw him at the Eckridge ranch."

"Are you crazy? Who?"

"Me."

"He'll never believe—"

"Just call him, Joe. Now."

TWENTY-TWO

JOANNA'S ASSUMPTION about Robert Donatello proved correct: It took very little persuasion on Joe's part to get him to agree to come to the winery. Joe hung up the phone in the tasting room looking sick and wandered back toward the lab. Joanna stuck with him, leaving Adam to contact Detective Lennon. When they'd stopped by the sheriff's department substation on their way to the winery, they'd explained the situation to him. He was standing by.

Back in the lab, Joe slumped in a chair, eyes closed. "Do you know how much I hate doing this?" he asked.

"I know." She sat down next to him. "Joe, there's something that's still bothering me. There're plenty of people in the business of arranging art thefts. Why did your grandfather contact Parducci?"

"That was another bad thing of my doing. My grandfather told me about the problem with the Van Gogh when the first items about the auction appeared. He was so distraught—Ronnie's political future would be destroyed, he said. The winery he'd struggled to build would suffer from the adverse publicity. He wouldn't be prosecuted, but he'd live out the rest of his days in disgrace. Our good name . . . well, you get the picture.

"I wasn't buying any of that shit. Ronnie's political position was achieved through dirty dealings; the winery was built with illegally obtained funds; my grandfather—well, I just said I couldn't help him. Then he came up with this scheme to have the painting stolen. He asked me if I knew anybody who could undertake it. I was pissed that he'd even think I knew that kind of people, and I broke a confidence and said he and E.J.'s real father would get along real well. After that he wouldn't let me alone until I agreed to ask E.J. how somebody would go about securing the services of someone like Parducci.

"We often talked about Parducci, E.J. and I. He was worried about your insistence that he was still alive. In the course of one of those conversations I asked how a person would contact Parducci about a job. E.J. thought it was a purely academic question, of course. He said if you asked among dealers and collectors, just dropped the name, eventually you'd connect with someone on the shady side who would put you in touch. I guess that's what my grandfather did." He sighed, as if he were winded by his long recital.

"Joe," she said, "*why* did you do all that for your grandfather? I know how you feel about him and Ronnie. And you were finally breaking away from them."

"Like I told you before, you don't understand what it's like to be a Donatello. My grandfather's an expert at emotional blackmail; he uses guilt the way other rich men use their money. Ever since our parents' plane crash, when only Ronnie and I survived, he's managed to make us feel guilty. We've always known he wishes we had died, rather than his only son.

"Ronnie was older than me when it happened, and the guilt really took hold on her. She's spent her life trying to be a replacement for our father. I resisted, but only in little ways. It took me until E.J. bought the winery to make the decision to get out from under the old man's thumb—and then I allowed him to suck me into this mess."

Adam's footsteps sounded outside the door to the living quarters. He gave them a thumbs-up sign. "I'm going to meet Lennon now."

Joe's eyes filled with alarm as Adam went out. "He's not going to bring that detective here, is he? I told you, my grandfather may not even talk with you—"

"The sheriff's men will wait until we have a confession."

Joe nodded, accepting what she'd hoped to imply. Moments later the sound of Adam's car leaving the parking area was audible. He would move it to a spot on the shoulder of the highway, she knew, then meet with Lennon and return on foot through the vineyard. Sheriff's department backup units would be in place to assist them.

As they waited, Joanna and Joe sat in silence. Her weary body hummed with tension. She reviewed the situation, went over the things she would say, the responses she hoped to get. If she could only get through this one last confrontation, then something might be salvaged....

Another car drove into the parking area. "That's him," Joe said.

"Go out to meet him. Don't worry about being nervous. It's normal under the circumstances." She watched him leave, then felt under the table for the bug Adam had planted while Joe called his grandfather. Adam and Lennon had had ample time to enter the winery and take up position in the tasting room with the tape recorder, but she had no way of knowing whether they were really there. "Wish me luck," she whispered.

Voices came from outside. Joe held the door open for his grandfather. The elder Donatello's face was haggard but composed; his windbreaker and freshly pressed slacks gave him the appearance of one who is on his way to play eighteen holes of golf.

"Mrs. Stark." He nodded. Then he looked around the room, eyes resting on the inside door. "I trust we're alone," he said to Joe.

Since Joe believed that to be true, his affirmative response was convincing.

Donatello moved toward the card table and sat opposite Joanna. He folded his hands on it and paused briefly before he spoke. "My grandson tells me you have been making preposterous allegations against me."

"I merely told him what I saw at the Eckridge ranch last night."

"And what was that?"

"You don't deny you were there?"

"Just tell me what you're claiming."

"That you shot Eckridge in the back, Donatello."

"That's ridiculous."

"Do you recall a car you forced into the ditch beside the driveway? A white Fiat convertible?"

Donatello started and nodded—involuntarily, almost imperceptibly.

Dammit! she thought. Say something out loud so they can get it on the tape!

"Does that mean yes?" she asked.

"What about this white Fiat?"

"I was the driver of the car. And I recognized you."

Silence. Donatello's face became immobile, but his eyes moved nervously about the room.

She said, "I saw you as you came at me."

"That isn't possible. It was dusky—"

Success! "I saw you. You were driving your Jaguar, I believe. You haven't had time to get it repainted; there are traces of the paint from my car on it—and from it on mine. The sheriff's department has impounded the Fiat, of course."

Donatello compressed his lips. After a moment he said, "What do you want, Mrs. Stark?"

"Does that mean you admit shooting Jerome Eckridge?"

"Get to the point, Mrs. Stark."

"For my own satisfaction, I want to know what happened with Eckridge."

The old man's eyes grew glacial, hard. "That you are not entitled to know. I will tell you one thing, as a warning: The man was greedy. I offered him a great deal of money not to reveal he had bought that painting from Davis Deane. Eckridge wouldn't take it."

"What about Deane? Did you think he would tell what the two of you engineered all those years ago?"

"I was certain."

"Because you'd had a falling-out."

"There was no falling-out. I merely cut Deane out of my life. After his wife died he became a drunk. He became fiscally irresponsible, as drunks are prone to do. Then he wanted me to bail him out. I refused; he was too far gone—no amount of help would have saved him at that point. Of course he reminded me of our mutual crime and said he would go to the authorities. I reminded *him* it was indeed a *mutual* crime, and that he was the one in possession of the stolen paintings. After that his demands ceased."

Anger rose inside Joanna: she struggled to contain it.

Donatello noticed. "You think me cold, Mrs. Stark?"

"I think you inhuman."

He shrugged. "That's your privilege. It won't stop us from doing business. How much do you want to keep silent about this?"

"Nothing."

His eyes narrowed.

"Not money, that is."

"What, then?"

She paused, looked up at Joe. He was staring at her in surprise, realizing she had deviated from the script she and Adam had outlined. Then she looked back at Donatello.

"My son is currently under suspicion of the murder of Antony Parducci," she said. "I want E.J. exonerated."

Donatello's white eyebrows drew together. "And how can I do that? I didn't kill Mr. Parducci. God knows I needed him alive."

"I know you didn't kill him. But you can give me the man who did."

Both Donatellos grew very still. Joanna felt her own breath catch. It was a full minute before the old man turned to his grandson.

"Joey," he said. "Joey."

Joe might have been one of the bronzes created by the sculptor who had borne the same name.

"Joey," his grandfather said, "we have to help the lady."

When Joe moved, it was only his eyes. They met Joanna's. Surprisingly they contained no anger, no fear—only the most profound sorrow.

"You knew," he said.

"I knew."

"Why didn't you just accuse me?"

She ignored the question, exhausted and anxious now to have it all in the open. "Tell me what happened."

". . . I did it for you. I did it for E.J."

"I knew that, too. Go on."

He stood with his eyes on hers for a longer moment. Then his gaze shifted to his grandfather. His face twisted with revulsion, and he moved farther away from the old man, toward Joanna. The shift in position was not lost on Donatello; he flinched and looked down at his hands.

"Friday afternoon," Joe began, "E.J. went back to your house and found a note from you saying you'd gone to San Francisco. That worried him, so he decided to go in after you. He called somebody he thought might be able to advise him about the Parducci business, like I told you. When he left here, he said he'd probably connect with you at the apartment.

"That worried *me*. I kept thinking about giving that key ring to my grandfather. I knew his whole story was a lie. I kept remembering Grandfather had been so eager to contact Parducci—and then just stopped talking about it. I kept thinking about the auction being the next day. But I didn't want to risk taking action, on the chance I was wrong."

"What changed that?"

"Something Karla said. She and I went to Ronnie's wine auction and then to dinner. By then I was more afraid than worried. I was going on about friendship—where its responsibilities start and stop. And Karla said—she'd had a close friend die recently—she said that they start the minute you know you're going to become friends and don't stop until death—of either the friend or the friendship. She said that having a friend die is terrible, but that the death of a friendship is even worse."

"She's a wise lady."

"Yes, she is. I took off and drove like hell to the city. When I got to your building, I followed another tenant inside. The apartment door was unlocked. There was a stranger there; I knew he had to be Parducci. He had a gun. He went crazy when he saw me. Dragged me inside. He was coming at me...those eyes...the man was insane. I grabbed one of the knives from the rack in the kitchen—"

Joe stood with his arms rigid, tears that he didn't bother to wipe away beginning to slide down his cheeks. "He was out of control. He stumbled before he could aim the gun. The knife...God help me...I put it into his chest...it went in like...oh shit it was awful, I had no idea what it would be like to—"

"You killed him in self-defense," Joanna said.

"I took a *life*. One minute he was moving and breathing and the next—"

"Self-defense, Joe."

He put his hands to his face and sobbed.

Robert Donatello had listened dispassionately to his grandson's confession. Now he said, "We've got to call the sheriff, Joey. I'll hire you the best defense attorney in the country. Don't worry about a thing."

Joanna stood up, feeling her lips draw back from her teeth, like those of an attacking animal. "You are a truly evil man, Donatello," she said. "You'd throw away your own grandson to save your skin. But that's not going to happen."

For a moment Donatello didn't seem to comprehend. Then the knowledge that this was a setup dawned in his eyes. He reared up, reached across the table, and shoved at her shoulders. She toppled into Joe; together they careened into the wall.

Joe pushed her away and started toward his grandfather. Joanna staggered, righted herself, and went after him.

Donatello had moved back by the outside door. He was reaching into the pocket of his windbreaker.

Jesus, she thought, *the gun!*

Joe realized that, too. He yelled "Don't!" and lunged at his grandfather.

Donatello sidestepped, the gun out of his pocket now.

Joe whirled, grabbed Joanna by the waist, and flung her to the floor. Her forehead smacked into the concrete. For a time she felt only confusion and gut-wrenching pain. The room was full of noise, other voices now. There had been no shot. When she finally raised her head she saw a blur of khaki uniforms. Someone—Lennon?—was droning on about the right to remain silent.

Someone else's hands helped her to a sitting position. Adam's voice said, "You okay?"

"What took you so long?" she asked groggily.

"That tasting room seemed to be miles away. Are you all right?"

She didn't reply; she was looking at Joe, who stood in the grip of one of the deputies. He said, ''Why'd you bring it to this, Jo? Why, with the cops listening?''

''I wanted it on tape,'' she said. ''I knew if it was, everyone would believe you. As I believed you. It's going to be okay now.''

TWENTY-THREE

JOANNA CROSSED the lobby of the old hotel and went to the glass doors to the courtyard. They had been relocked since she'd left some ten hours before. She turned the key and went outside. The court was bathed in the hard white light of noon; it spilled down through the cracked and shattered greenhouse roof onto the mounded debris in the pool. Without hesitation she went to a point near the far end, knelt down, and began removing the scraps of wood, miscellaneous pieces of metal, broken flower pots and crockery and bottles.

It was hot in the refracted light. Some of the debris was heavy and cumbersome; other pieces were wedged tight. She worked steadily—feeling somewhat rested after catching a couple of hours' sleep—tossing the smaller objects helter-skelter around her. Occasionally she stopped to glance at the hotel and wipe sweat from her brow. The excavating took longer than she'd expected, but finally she uncovered what she was seeking: a tarpaulin-wrapped object about two feet square.

She climbed down into the depression she'd made and lifted the bundle, setting it gently on the side of the pool. Then she scrambled up beside it and unwrapped the tarp. Inside was a wooden crate of the kind used to protect artworks in transit. She looked for a tool, found a rusted kitchen knife in the scattered trash, and pried the crate open.

Still more wrappings—brown paper this time. She lifted out what they protected and tore the paper free. The painting was even more impressive than she'd imagined. She whistled softly in surprise.

The Vineyard at Marmande had more substance than its sister painting. The terraced hillside it depicted rose almost like the waves of a stormy sea. The greens, blues, yellows, and purples were rich and vivid; the brushstrokes were short and harsh. There was a fierce energy trapped on the canvas, as if Van Gogh had used it to expunge his rage at his debilitating madness. Joanna stared at the painting for a long time, then covered it with the tarp and sat down on the edge of the pool, her feet dangling above the depression she'd dug.

A movement drew her attention to the half-open glass doors. She looked over there and smiled as E.J. stepped out.

"It's about time," she said. "I could have used your help."

He came all the way into the courtyard and looked around. "What's this?"

"I came to rescue something belonging to Davis Deane." She pulled back the tarp and showed him the Van Gogh.

He whistled the same way she had.

"So where have you been?" She patted the concrete beside her. "Lurking upstairs?"

"Yeah." He sat next to her, dangling his feet, too. "Wondering who it was *this* time. For someplace that's supposed to be abandoned, it's been as busy as a BART station here. Finally I decided to check it out, saw it was only you."

"If you'd checked it out when I was here last night, you might have saved me some trouble."

"That was you then, too? Shit, I thought it was the cops, so I hid in this cubbyhole I'd made for myself on the second floor." He smiled wryly. "Of course it occurred to me afterward that the cops generally announce themselves. Will you please tell me what's going on?"

"First you tell me what happened. I assume you found Parducci's body at my apartment."

"Yeah. Jesus. I'd stopped there first to change my clothes before I met Nick for dinner—"

"Nick! The one person I couldn't reach to ask if he'd seen you. I talked with him earlier that afternoon, though, and he didn't mention you had a date."

"I asked him not to. I thought maybe he could help me decide what to do. Of course I realized early on that it was a mistake; even after I told him everything, he still seemed to think your fears of Parducci were exaggerated."

"Were you with him all that time—until after two?"

"Yeah. It was a late dinner; we didn't even meet until nine. Then he wanted to go have drinks and talk some more. He kept lecturing me on how I should get you to see a psychiatrist. I didn't get back to the apartment until nearly two-thirty and, Jesus, Jo, the blood. It was all over my down jacket that I'd left on the couch. I couldn't make myself touch the thing. The man was a monster, but—"

"But he was your father."

"My father." His mouth twisted bitterly.

"It was bad for me, too—in spite of all the things he'd done."

"Yes. Well. The window was open, like somebody had left by the fire escape. I panicked and went out that way, too. I was worried about you, and didn't know where to look, so I tore back here to the house. When I couldn't find you there, I went to the winery and told Joe what had happened. He said I ought to lie low until he could find out what was going on. He had keys to this place, so we ditched my bike and he brought me here."

"And he found out the police were looking for you, so you stayed."

"Yes. He came a couple of times and brought me food and news. He said you were in the clear, but we decided it was better you didn't know where I was until they found the killer. I take it they have."

"Yes." Joanna related the events of the past days, silencing him when he tried to raise questions, in order not to go off on tangents. As she spoke E.J. looked incredulous, then angry, then sad.

When she finished, he said, "That Robert Donatello is one fuckin' bastard, isn't he? Poor Joe."

"You're not angry with him for lying to you and putting you through this?"

"A little, maybe. But I know what a bind he was in. What do you suppose'll happen to him?"

"I've already spoken with my lawyer. She says he can plead voluntary manslaughter. It's likely he'll get off with a light sentence. Of course, his future with the winery is up to you."

"We'll work that out, don't worry." E.J. was silent for a moment, then gestured at the Van Gogh. "Old man Deane had this hidden here all those years?"

"Yes. I suspected it was somewhere in the hotel, because of the burglar alarm, but I never thought of the pool. He was better this morning, and I got to see him for a few minutes. He told me where it was."

"And you say it wasn't Joe or his grandfather who ran him off the road the other night?"

"No one did. Deane admitted that this morning. He'd been up in Glen Ellen, trying to get hold of Jerry Eckridge and warn him that someone might try to steal the Van Gogh. He figured that Parducci would be apprehended, I'd be out of danger, and nothing else would have to come out. Only he was drunk and couldn't even find the ranch he used to own. Then on the way home he put himself in the ditch. It was just his old man's pride that made him claim someone had forced him off the road. Now he says he's going to do his drinking at home—and quit driving."

E.J. smiled faintly. "If they don't prosecute him for helping Donatello defraud his insurance company."

"Statute of limitations has run out on that. Of course, it makes Deane look bad, but I sense he's not a man who cares what people think any more."

"So the painting belongs to him?"

"He has possession. Maybe he'll let Adam auction it. It would buy, as Adam likes to say, a whole lotta lentils."

E.J. frowned. "What's with you and this Hawthorne character, anyway? Do I detect a romance in the works?"

"Don't get excited. Adam's a lot like David. In a way that's good, but he also has the same hyper quality. He doesn't know how to relax any more than David did—and you know how that used to drive me crazy. Besides, he spends a lot of time on his ranch, riding."

"What's wrong with that?"

"I'm afraid of horses."

"Oh, right. Well, it'll be interesting to see what develops."

Joanna ignored the comment and began rewrapping the Van Gogh.

"What're you going to do with that?" E.J. asked.

"Deliver it to Karla Perelli. Deane told Sally Jane I should take the painting to her if he didn't make it through surgery. Now it appears he wants her to have it anyway." She paused and yawned. "After I drop this off at her place, I'm going to bed and sleep for a week." With an effort, she started to get up.

E.J. remained seated on the edge of the pool. "I've been thinking—about you and me," he said. "We're free, you know. No more fear, no more possibility of Parducci stepping into our lives and wrecking them."

"I've thought of that, too."

"What're you going to do with all that freedom, Jo?"

She sat back down and considered the question. "I'm not sure. You know I'm not one for making sweeping changes." After a moment she smiled tentatively. "Now, little changes—*those* I can deal with. What would you think of us taking a trip back east, to see your grandfather and his wife?''

"Sounds like an idea whose time has come."

"As I said, it's only a little change."

"A little change that'll pave the way for the bigger ones."

EPILOGUE

On April 28, 1988, Joe Donatello pleaded guilty to the voluntary manslaughter of Antony Parducci and received a five-year suspended sentence. He has since resumed his duties as winemaker at the Elliot J. Stark Vineyards.

Robert Donatello was indicted for the first-degree murder of Jerome Eckridge on May 11, 1988. He died of a stroke on June 18, while awaiting trial.

After being overwhelmingly defeated in her bid for the United States House of Representatives, Veronica Donatello claimed to have withdrawn from politics. However, a recent telephone poll of registered voters in Sonoma County, financed by former Donatello backers, indicates she may be planning a comeback at the local level.

Tokaido International, the Japanese insurance firm that was the successful bidder for *Flowers along the Rhone*, decided to accept the painting in spite of its clouded provenance. It now hangs in the company's museum in Tokyo.

Davis Deane has fully recovered from his injuries. He has consistently refused to sell *The Vineyard at Marmande*, and the painting currently hangs in the living room of the home owned by his great-granddaughter Karla Perelli. Deane still lives alone in his cabin at Madrone Springs Resort. These days, Karla is welcome to sit on his porch with him at any time—provided she arrives bearing a fifth of Jim Beam.

Elliot J. Stark Vineyards' 1988 Private Reserve Chardonnay was awarded a gold medal at the prestigious Intervin competition, held in New York in early April, 1989. The vintner celebrated by temporarily turning over his responsibilities to his winemaker in order that he might take a three-week backpacking trip through New England in the company of a young woman whom he met during the competition.

Joanna Stark and Adam Hawthorne were married in a civil ceremony at the Stark Vineyards on May 20, 1989. Among the attendees were the bride's father and stepmother, John and Millie Scherer of Tenafly, New Jersey. Joanna and Adam divide their time between their San Francisco home, their Marin County ranch (where she is learning to ride), and their farmhouse in Sonoma (where he is learning to relax). Mrs. Hawthorne's company, Security Systems International, is now solidly in the black, as a result of having secured the Renfrow's Auctioneers account.